THE AI

**Katherine Mansfield**
Katherine Mansfield (1888-1923) was born in Wellington, New Zealand, but moved to Europe in 1903. In London she befriended avant garde writers such as D.H. Lawrence, Virginia Woolf and the critic John Middleton Murry. Her own work, influenced by Anton Chekhov, made her name as a master of stories and short fiction.

New Zealand-born **Kirsty Gunn** is the author of five novels, *The Boy and the Sea, Featherstone, Rain, The Keepsake* and *This Place You Return To Is Home*, and a collection of her own writings and poems, *44 Things*. She lives with her family in London and Dundee, where she directs the writing programme for the University.

# The Aloe

# The Aloe

---

## Katherine Mansfield

FOREWORD BY KIRSTY GUNN

Original text edited by Vincent O'Sullivan

CAPUCHIN CLASSICS

CAPUCHIN CLASSICS
LONDON

The Aloe

First published by Capuchin Classics in 2010
© Capuchin Classics 2010
Transcription copyright Vincent O'Sullivan 1982, 1985

2 4 6 8 0 9 7 5 3 1

Capuchin Classics
128 Kensington Church Street, London W8 4BH
Telephone: +44 (0)20 7221 7166
Fax: +44 (0)20 7792 9288
E-mail: info@capuchin-classics.co.uk
www.capuchin-classics.co.uk

*Châtelaine of Capuchin Classics*: Emma Howard

ISBN: 978-1-9074290-8-8

Vincent O'Sullivan's transcription of the text of
*The Aloe* has been edited to omit those lines and
words deleted by Katherine Mansfield in her
original manuscript.

"...and the top of the cream jar flew through the air and rolled like a penny in a round on the linoleum and did not break. But for Kezia it had broken the moment it flew through the air and she picked it up, hot all over, put it on the dressing table and walked away, *far* too quickly – and airily."

So ends *The Aloe*, New Zealand-born writer Katherine Mansfield's brightly finished picture of domestic life at the turn of the last century as seen through the clarifying lens of memory...And something has been broken. Just as for Kezia the lid of the jar has come apart "the moment it flew through the air", so what is caught here, in words, is a thing of fragments, held together as though by chance but never really whole. For the past from which this story is made, Katherine Mansfield's past, her New Zealand past, her Wellington past, has been broken with long ago. They are the shattered pieces of it you are now holding in your hand.

Of course, for Mansfield, the great practitioner of the sliver, the "slice of life", the European short story, the idea of pieces comes as no surprise. Her narratives were always made as parts and scenes and tiny, cleanly cut-out unremarkable dramas. But nowhere else in her work is the sense of fracture more apparent than in *The Aloe*, nowhere else does she so accommodate such broken-up content. Here is a kind of fiction that, more than the other stories, celebrates, delights in and puts forward for our notice, a different way of reading – a way of seeing, actually – that means one can only regard the piece in separate incidents in order to have it at all. The vivid, disparate scenes seem to be set down randomly, just as they occur to the author, like life happening on the page, with memory and sudden thought converging and no sense of dramatic intent or overbearing structure to hold any of it artificially in place. The reader simply looks on, as witness and participant, as the story moves us in and out of rooms and conversations, stopping here for a cup of tea, there to look at a flower. We come up too close, sometimes, to recollection, moments of family history, and we meet new characters only to leave them again and return to what is familiar, going back out into the garden with the little sisters and cousins to get some fresh air...

"What form is it? you ask..." Katherine Mansfield wrote in letters referring to her new literary project. "As far as I know it's more or less my own invention."[1]

It is easy to see how that "invention" caught Virginia Woolf's eye, reflecting as it does in bright fragments her own "moments of being" and resulting in the publication by Woolf's Hogarth Press in 1917 of the edited and cut-back *Aloe*, the story that we know today as *Prelude*.[2] Both versions are profound, highly wrought examples of a still emerging Modernist English tradition that placed aesthetics and the arrangement of images and ideas over traditional narrative methods, and *Prelude*, Mansfield's shorter and more precise version of the original, is without doubt the greater artistic achievement.

But in *The Aloe* we see more intensely than in that second more polished work the very processes of an artist discovering her aesthetic through necessity; by making good something that is no longer whole, no longer available to her, that she may have it back, somehow, all the scattered bits returned in one piece. "Oh, I want for one moment to make our undiscovered country leap into the eyes of the Old World," she wrote in her journal, while getting the beginnings of her new story down. "It must be mysterious, as though floating. It must take the breath...But all must be told with a sense of mystery..."[3] And, she wrote later, "in a special kind of prose".

It is what I might call "psychic imperative", this need to find a new method, a new literary style that can cope with the sheer complexities of a work's emotional and psychological content –

and we see it present in all examples of great literature, from *To the Lighthouse* to *War and Peace*, like a deeply humming engine sitting within the brand new design that has been created to fit perfectly around it. So Mansfield wrote this book far, far away from the house and garden in which it is set, on the other side of the world, with the recent death of her beloved brother Leslie, who'd been killed in the War, fresh in her mind – another break there, another fracture – but all the memories of the time they'd had together when they were children "at home" come back to her to energise and breathe life into her project. And far from it being an incomplete version, a mere first draft, *The Aloe* fully defines how Mansfield finds in the fragment not something broken off, deranged and unfinished, but the very beginning of the story, the start of everything she needs.

Her own life, ever since leaving New Zealand for the first time, as a schoolgirl, was a restless, interrupted affair – going from place to place, back to New Zealand, then to London again, from London to Germany to France to Italy and back to France… She was never settled. She lived in hotel rooms and short-rent apartments, shuttling between cities and the country, staying with friends, and finally, her body spent and wrecked by tuberculosis, finishing up in a quasi-religious institute that was only half-built and where, even then, in the last weeks of her life, she was moved from one room to another as though to be in one place ever for any length of time was to be denied her.

Yet *The Aloe* gives us a very different kind of story. It is assured, comfortable, and deeply comforting – as though the author has never left home, as though her brother and sisters are with her, as though she is safe. And we as readers are plunged into the family life of the Fairfields as though we too have always belonged there. So we move with them from town to the country – and though there may be some uncertainties about the new life they have chosen, with the mother Linda's dreamy melancholy unable to find expression in the sunlit garden and rooms full of the sounds of people calling, and though Linda's younger sister Beryl confides to a friend in a letter that she think she may "rot" there away from society and its diversions, still there is nothing uncertain about the solidity of the home, of its seductions and claustrophobia, its horrors and longueurs.

In Kezia, the young girl who appears throughout Mansfield's work, whose character seems to guide us through the story, there is nothing fractured either. Only the deliciousness instead of waking with her in the morning to hear the birds singing and to see the light creeping across the wall... Of going into the kitchen after hanging paintings on new walls to have a cup of tea and a slice of gingerbread with the Grandmother who has laid it all out there nicely on a linen cloth...

This is Katherine Mansfield making a "home for herself in words", to paraphrase a line taken from the cultural and literary critic Edward Said when he's describing what it is to be a writer.[4] She is bringing together her broken life that is spread in bits about the world, the memories of her dead brother and her estranged family, all gathered into one house, one place, one time. It's as though the pieces of her past are allowed to make a pattern then, one vivid part laid next to another, background and foreground in one. Here at one corner is the bright garden, at another the mysterious horse-and-cart ride through the streets at night as the little girls leave their city home for the house in the hills. Here is Pat the handyman coming along with his axe to take the head off a white duck, here is the Grandmother sleeping softly next to her favourite grandchild. One scene after another falling into place as the writer takes each moment and sets it next to another, creating in that "special prose" a story of fragments and scenes – one would not even call them "chapters" – as a sort of mosaic, or better, re-conjoined in much the same way as a cleanly fractured ceramic may have all its shards fitted together and presented again as a whole. So we are meant to see the cracks, I think, and to find them just as lovely.

For those who admire Mansfield's work, the avid reader or student of writing, this Capuchin volume, taken from Vincent O'Sullivan's edition of the comparative texts of the two stories first published in 1982 and then singly as *The Aloe* in 1985,[5] allows us full access to Mansfield's creative mind. For one can compare this earlier version with the later, shorter *Prelude* and get a real sense of how she went to work on her story, of those scenes that were first scribbled down in bits in a child's exercise book in London and in France. To see that writing, the pen moving so fast one can barely make out the letters of the words, is to see how the structure came together quite clearly for this writer as something made in fragments, how the fragments bore her away...One might barely conceive at times that they would ever become any kind of joined together book or novella. A vision of that way of making a story, a kind of piece-work, remains in the published form of *The Aloe*, with all the words in it given over to considering the life that Katherine Mansfield had once known so well, those detailed scenes crammed with remembered New Zealand details, its bush and plants and native birds...And how rich and rewarding it is to read the two stories side by side, to see what was taken and what was left, to regard first hand the burgeoning writing imagination before the editing mind comes in to prune and clear and cut away.

There is an "abandonment to the leisurely rhythm of her own imagination" wrote Rebecca West of Mansfield's New Zealand stories, of which *The Aloe* is the most concentrated as well as the most extensive example. It's as though the ideas have lived so long in her mind that she can "ransack them for the difficult, rare, essential points".[6] And indeed in the scenes that remain here, that are gone from *Prelude*, it is as though Mansfield, in her writing, has built her house of words with as many rooms as she can to move around in, so she can discover later where best to stand to hold the light, the shadow... Only then will she find out that she doesn't need to use all of her initial construction – but somehow it must be there at her back for now, as she starts out in her enterprise, to give ballast, the balance and sense of reality upon which to base her art.

Towards the end of her short life Mansfield turned repeatedly to the subject of what was "real"[7], in her search for wholeness, unity, a melding of the spiritual and practical, her personality and her literary sensibility – a drive that Vincent O'Sullivan has described as existential in nature, and one that had her seeking the elemental, the necessary, as she sought to make peace with her past and present, to reconcile the self she represented to the world with her inner secret being, the one still inevitably connected with her home, her birthplace and her beginning and whom, he shows us, she came to inhabit in her best work and at the end of her life.[8]

In this book, her first committed attempt to begin that reconciliation as she starts to gather up these aspects of her past and get it all down in words, we find her claiming the thing she sought so desperately in those last months of her life – and in it shines the singularity of her art. Her broken world is made whole again. In the shattered parts of *The Aloe* we find the "real".

*Kirsty Gunn*
*Thorndon, Wellington 2009*

Notes and Further Reading

1. Katherine Mansfield's letters and journals give us vivid insights to her literary and creative processes. The "invention" that is the form of *The Aloe* is taken from the following passage:

"What form is it? you ask...As far as I know it's more or less my own invention. And how have I shaped it? This is about as much as I can say about it. You know, if the truth were known I have a perfect passion for the island where I was born...Well in the early morning there I always remember feeling that this little island had dipped back into the dark blue sea during the night only to rise again at beam of day, all hung with bright spangles and glittering drops... I tried to catch that moment – with something of that sparkle and its flavour. And just as on those mornings white milky mists rise and uncover some beauty, then smother it again and then again disclose it. I tried to lift that mist from my people and let them be seen and then to hide them again."

From *The Letters of Katherine Mansfield*, 1903-1917, ed Vincent O'Sullivan and Margaret Scott, Oxford University Press 1984, p. 331

2. A comparative edition of *The Aloe and Prelude* was published by The Port Nicholson Press, Wellington, New Zealand in 1982 and Carcanet New Press, Manchester in 1983, showing clearly where cuts were made in the text, paragraphs eliminated, words changed and so on – and so describing, page by page, how Mansfield created a lighter, less obviously autobiographical *Prelude* from her more definitively "colonial" New Zealand original.

For a deft and important account of the literary relationship between Virginia Woolf and Katherine Mansfield, about whom Woolf wrote "I was jealous of her writing – the only writing I have ever been jealous of", see Angela Smith's *Katherine Mansfield and Virginia Woolf: A Public of Two* (1999) which sets the writers side by side and uses their letters and journals (both were keen on both) to delineate similarities and differences.

3. When Mansfield's beloved younger brother Leslie was killed in the First World War, Mansfield's grief turned her back to the past. She vowed in her journal to create a kind of memorial to the dead boy in her writing – "the only

possible value that anything can have for me is that it should put me in mind of something that happened when we were alive," she wrote. This creative desire, to make life out of death was the impulse that generated *The Aloe* and Mansfield is addressing Leslie directly when she ends the passage quoted in the introduction "But all must be told with a sense of mystery, a radiance, and afterglow, because you, my little sun, are set."

From *Journal of Katherine Mansfield*, ed John Middleton Murray, 1962, pp 89, 94

4. Edward Said has written in his memoir that a writer is most always "an outsider, nomadic, somehow, in temperament – and that no matter where he or she lives or for how long it is only in writing, in each attempt at a story, at a poem or a piece of text, that he or she can make something fixed in the midst of uncertainty, create a place of safety, be at home".

Taken from the Introduction to *Out of Place* by Edward Said, Granta, 2000

5. Rebecca West was a great admirer of Katherine Mansfield's work and wrote with keen perception about Mansfield's "poetic temperament" as it applied to her creation of characters and setting in a review of *The Garden Party*:

"Abandonment to the leisurely rhythm of her own imagination, and refusal to conform to the current custom and finish her book in a year's session, has enabled her to bring her inventions right over the threshold of art. They are extraordinarily solid; they have lived so long in her mind that she knows all about them and can ransack them for the difficult, rare, essential points."

From the *New Statesman* 18 March 1922: 678. Reprinted in *Katherine Mansfield's Selected Stories*, ed Vincent O'Sullivan, Norton, 2006

6. Katherine Mansfield died of tuberculosis in 1923 when she was 35. As her illness worsened, her need to find a place for herself in the world that might be safe and give her comfort, that might allow her to feel somehow authentic and honest and true…This instinct crystallised in her use of the word "real" – "If I were allowed one single cry to God that cry would be: *I want to be* REAL," she wrote in December 1922, a month before her death.

From *The Collected Letters of Katherine Mansfield*, ed Vincent O'Sullivan and Margaret Scott, Oxford, 2008, p. 341

7. For a poignant and finely tuned account of Mansfield's last years, describing the writer's sense of herself as an artist in search of an honest account of herself and her work before her death, see Vincent O'Sullivan's introduction to the above volume – the last broken lines of which, taken from a list of Mansfield's notes of Russian phrases and words, is itself testament to the keen beauty, emotional truth and wholeness of a fragmented literary sensibility: "I was late because my fire did not burn…The sky was blue as in summer…The trees still have apples. Apple…I fed the goats…I go for a walk…What is the time. Time."

## Publisher's Note

The text as it appears in this edition is taken directly from Mansfield's original notebooks.

# Chapter One

There was not an inch of room for Lottie and Kezia in the buggy. When Pat swung them on top of the luggage they wobbled; the Grandmother's lap was full and Linda Burnell could *not possibly* have held a lump of a child on hers for such a distance. Isabel, very superior perched beside Pat on the driver's seat. Hold-alls, bags, and band boxes were piled upon the floor.

"These are *absolute* necessities that I will not let out of my sight for *one instant*," said Linda Burnell, her voice trembling with fatigue and over excitement.

Lottie and Kezia stood on the patch of lawn just inside the gate all ready for the fray in their reefer coats with brass anchor buttons and little round caps with battle ship ribbons. Hand in hand. They stared with round inquiring eyes first at the "absolute necessities" and then at their Mother.

"We shall simply have to leave them. That is all. We shall simply have to cast them off" said Linda Burnell. A strange little laugh flew from her lips; she leaned back upon the buttoned leather cushions and shut her eyes . . . laughing silently.

Happily, at that moment, Mrs Samuel Josephs, who lived next door and had been watching the scene from behind her drawing room blind, rustled down the garden path.

"Why nod leave the children with *be* for the afterdoon, Brs Burnell. They could go on the dray with the storeban when he comes in the eveding. Those thigs on the path have to go. Dodn't they?"

"Yes, everything outside the house has to go," said Linda Burnell, waving a white hand at the tables and chairs that stood, impudently, on their heads in front of the empty house.

"Well, dodn't you worry, Brs Burnell. Loddie and Kezia can have tea with by children and I'll see them safely on the dray afterwards."

She leaned her fat, creaking body across the gate and smiled reassuringly. Linda Burnell pretended to consider.

"Yes, it really is quite the best plan. I am *extremely* obliged to you, Mrs Samuel Josephs, I'm *sure*. Children, say 'Thank you' to Mrs Samuel Josephs." . . .

(Two subdued chirrups: "Thank you, Mrs Samuel Josephs.")

"And be good obedient little girls and – come closer –" – they advanced – "do not forget to tell Mrs Samuel Josephs when you want to" . . .

"Yes, Mother."

"Dodn't worry, Brs Burnell."

At the last moment Kezia let go Lottie's hand and darted towards the buggy.

"I want to kiss Grandma 'good-bye' again." Her heart was bursting.

"Oh, *dear* me!" wailed Linda Burnell.

But the grandmother leant her charming head in the lilac flowery bonnet towards Kezia and when Kezia searched her face she said – "It's alright, my darling. Be good." The buggy rolled off up the road, Isabel, proudly sitting by Pat, her nose turned up at all the world, Linda Burnell, prostrate, and crying behind her veil, and the Grandmother rumminaging among the curious oddments she had put in her black silk reticule at the last moment for lavender smelling salts to give her daughter.

The buggy twinkled away in the sunlight and fine golden dust – up the hill and over. Kezia bit her lip hard, but Lottie, carefully finding her handkerchief first, set up a howl.

"Mo-ther! Gran'*ma*!"

Mrs Samuel Josephs, like an animated black silk tea-cosey, waddled to Lottie's rescue.

"It's alright, by dear. There-there, ducky! Be a brave child. You come and blay in the nursery."

She put her arm round weeping Lottie and led her away. Kezia followed, making a face at Mrs Samuel Josephs' placket, which was undone *as* usual with two long pink corset laces hanging out of it.

The Samuel Josephs were not a family. They were a swarm. The moment you entered the house they cropped up and jumped out at you from under the tables, through the stair rails, behind the doors, behind the coats in the passage. Impossible to count them: impossible to distinguish between them. Even in the family groups that Mrs Samuel Josephs caused to be taken twice yearly – herself and Samuel in the middle – Samuel with parchment roll clenched on knee and she with the youngest girl on hers – you never could be sure how many children really were there. You counted them and then you saw another head or another small boy in a white sailor suit perched on the arm of a basket chair. All the girls were fat, with black hair tied up in red ribbons and eyes like buttons. The little ones had scarlet faces but the big ones were white with blackheads and dawning moustaches. The boys had the same jetty hair, the same button eyes but they were further adorned with ink black finger nails. (The girls bit theirs, so the black didn't show.) And every single one of them started a pitched battle as soon as possible after birth with every single other.

When Mrs Samuel Josephs was not turning up their clothes or down their clothes (as the sex might be) and beating them with a hair brush she called this pitched battle "airing their lungs". She seemed to take a pride in it and to bask in it from far away like a fat General watching through field glasses his troops in violent action . . .

Lottie's weeping died down as she ascended the Samuel Josephs' stairs, but the sight of her at the nursery door with swollen eyes and a blob of a nose gave great satisfaction to the S.J.'s, who sat on two benches before a long table covered with american cloth and set out with immense platters of bread and dripping and two brown jugs that faintly steamed.

"Hullo! You've been crying!"

"Ooh! Your eyes have gone right in!"

"Doesn't her nose look funny!"

"You're all red-an'-patchy!"

Lottie was quite a success. She felt it and swelled, smiling timidly.

"Go and sit by Zaidee, ducky," said Mrs Samuel Josephs, "and Kezia – you sit at the end by Boses."

Moses grinned and pinched her behind as she sat down but she pretended to take no notice. She did hate boys!

"Which will you have," asked Stanley, (a big one,) leaning across the table very politely and smiling at Kezia. "Which will you have to begin with – Strawberries and cream or bread and dripping?"

"Strawberries and cream, please," said she.

"Ah-h-h!" How they all laughed and beat the table with their tea spoons. Wasn't that a take in! Wasn't it! Wasn't it now! Didn't he fox her! Good old Stan!

"Ma! She thought it was real!"

Even Mrs Samuel Josephs, pouring out the milk and water, smiled indulgently. It was a merry tea.

After tea the young Samuel Josephs were turned out to grass until summoned to bed by their servant girl standing in the yard and banging on a tin tray with a potato masher.

"Know what we'll do," said Miriam. "Let's go an play hide-and-seek all over Burnells. Their back door is still open because they haven't got the side board out yet. I heard Ma tell Glad Eyes *she* wouldn't take such ole rubbish to a new house! Come on! Come on!"

"No, I don't want to," said Kezia, shaking her head.

"Ooh! Don't be soft. Come – do!"

Miriam caught hold of one of her hands; Zaidee snatched at the other.

"I don't not want to either, if Kezia doesn't," said Lottie, standing firm. But she, too, was whirled away . . . Now the whole fun of the game for the S.J.s was that the Burnell kids didn't want to play. In the yard they paused. Burnells' yard was small and square with flower beds on either side. All down one side big clumps of arum lilies aired their rich beauty, on the other side there was nothing but a straggle of what the children called "grandmother's pin cushions", a dull, pinkish flower, but so strong it would push its way and grow through a crack of concrete.

"You've only got one w. at your place," said Miriam scornfully. "We've got two at ours. One for men and one for ladies. The one for men hasn't got a seat."

"Hasn't got a seat!" cried Kezia. "I *don't* believe you."

"It's-true-it's-true-it's true! Isn't it Zaidee?" And Miriam began to dance and hop showing her flannelette drawers.

"Course it is," said Zaidee. "Well, you *are* a baby, Kezia!"

"I don't not believe it either if Kezia doesn't," said Lottie, after a pause.

But they never paid any attention to what Lottie said. Alice Samuel Josephs tugged at a lily leaf, twisted it off, turned it over. It was covered on the under side with tiny blue and grey snails.

"How much does your Pa give you for collecting snails," she demanded.

"Nothing!" said Kezia.

"Reely! Doesn't he give you anything? Our Pa gives us ha'penny a hundred. We put them in a bucket with salt and they all go bubbly like spittle. Don't you get any pocket money?"

"Yes, I get a penny for having my hair washed," said Kezia.

"An' a penny a tooth," said Lottie, softly.

"My! Is that *all*! One day Stanley took the money out of all our money boxes and Pa was so mad he rang up the police station."

"No, he didn't. Not reely," said Zaidee. "He only took the telephone down an spoke in it to frighten Stan."

"Ooh, you fibber! Ooh, you are a fibber," screamed Alice, feeling her story totter. "But Stan was so frightened he caught hold of Pa and screamed and bit him and then he lay on the floor and banged with his head as hard as ever."

"Yes," said Zaidee, warming. "And at dinner when the door bell rang an' Pa said to Stan – 'There they are – they've come for you –' do you know what Stan did?" Her button eyes snapped with joy. "He was sick – all over the table!"

"How perfeckly *horrid*," said Kezia, but even as she spoke she had one of her "ideas". It frightened her so that her knees trembled but it made her so happy she nearly screamed aloud with joy.

"Know a new game," said she. "All of you stand in a row and each person holds a narum lily head. I count one – two – three and when 'three' comes all of you have to bite out the yellow bit and scrunch it up – and who swallows first – wins."

The Samuel Josephs suspected nothing. They liked the game. A game where something had to be destroyed always fetched them. Savagely they broke off the big white blooms and stood in a row before Kezia.

"Lottie can't play," said Kezia.

But any way it didn't matter. Lottie was still patiently bending a lily head this way and that – it would not come off the stem for her.

"One – two – three," said Kezia.

She flung up her hands with joy as the Samuel Josephs bit, chewed, made dreadful faces, spat, screamed, and rushed to

Burnells' garden tap. But that was no good – only a trickle came out. Away they sped, yelling.

"Ma! Ma! Kezia's poisoned us."

"Ma! Ma! Me tongue's burning off."

"Ma! Ooh, Ma!"

"Whatever *is* the matter," asked Lottie, mildly, still twisting the frayed, oozing stem. "Kin I bite my lily off like this, Kezia?"

"No, silly." Kezia caught her hand. "It burns your tongue like anything."

"Is that why they all ran away," said Lottie. She did not wait for an answer. She drifted to the front of the house and began to dust the chair legs on the lawn with a corner of her pinafore.

Kezia felt very pleased. Slowly she walked up the back steps and through the scullery into the kitchen. Nothing was left in it except a lump of gritty yellow soap in one corner of the window sill and a piece of flannel stained with a blue bag in another. The fireplace was choked with a litter of rubbish. She poked among it for treasure but found nothing except a hair tidy with a heart painted on it that had belonged to the servant girl. Even that she left lying, and she slipped through the narrow passage into the drawing room. The Venetian blind was pulled down but not drawn close. Sunlight, piercing the green chinks, shone once again upon the purple urns brimming over with yellow chrysanthemums that patterned the walls – The hideous box was quite bare, so was the dining room except for the side board that stood in the middle, forlorn, its shelves edged with a scallop of black leather. But this room had a "funny" smell. Kezia lifted her head and sniffed again, to remember. Silent as a kitten she crept up the ladderlike stairs. In Mr and Mrs Burnell's room she found a pill box, black and shiny outside and red in, holding a blob of cotton wool. "I could keep a bird's egg in that," she decided.

The only other room in the house (the little tin bathroom did not count) was *their* room where Isabel and Lottie had slept in one bed and she and Grandma in another. She knew there was nothing there – she had watched Grandma pack – Oh, yes, there was! A stay button stuck in a crack of the floor and in another crack some beads and a long needle. She went over to the window and leaned against it pressing her hands against the pane.

From the window you saw beyond the yard a deep gully filled with tree ferns and a thick tangle of wild green, and beyond that there stretched the esplanade bounded by a broad stone wall against which the sea chafed and thundered. (Kezia had been born in that room. She had come forth squealing out of a reluctant mother in the teeth of a "Southerly Buster". The Grandmother, shaking her before the window had seen the sea rise in green mountains and sweep the esplanade – The little house was like a shell to its loud booming. Down in the gully the wild trees lashed together and big gulls wheeling and crying skimmed past the misty window.)

Kezia liked to stand so before the window. She liked the feeling of the cold shining glass against her hot little palms and she liked to watch the funny white tops that came on her fingers when she pressed them hard against the pane –

As she stood the day flickered out and sombre dusk entered the empty house, thievish dusk stealing the shapes of things, sly dusk painting the shadows. At her heels crept the wind, snuffling and howling. The windows shook – a creaking came from the walls and floors, a piece of loose iron on the roof banged forlornly – Kezia did not notice these things severally but she was suddenly quite, quite still with wide open eyes and knees pressed together – terribly frightened. Her old bogey, the dark, had overtaken her, and now there was no lighted room to make a despairing dash for – useless to call "Grandma" – useless to wait for the servant girl's cheerful stumping up the stairs to pull down the blinds and light the bracket lamp . . . There was only Lottie in the garden.  If she began to call Lottie *now* and went on calling her loudly all the while she flew downstairs and out of the house she might escape from *It* in time – It was round like the sun. It had a face. *It* smiled, but *It* had no eyes. *It* was yellow. When she was put to bed with two drops of aconite in the medicine glass *It* breathed very loudly and firmly and *It* had been known on certain particularly fearful occasions to turn round and round. *It* hung in the air. That was all she knew and even that much had been very difficult to explain to the Grandmother. Nearer came the terror and more plain to feel the "silly" smile. She snatched her hands from the window pane, opened her mouth to call Lottie, and fancied that she did call loudly, though she made no sound . . .*It* was at the top of the stairs; *It* was at the bottom of the stairs, waiting in the little dark passage, guarding the back door – But Lottie was at the back door, too.

"Oh, there you are," she said cheerfully. "The storeman's here. Everything's on the dray – and *three* horses, Kezia – Mrs Samuel Josephs has given us a big shawl to wear round us, and she says button up your coat. She won't come out because of asthma, and she says 'never do it again'" – Lottie was very important –

"Now then, you kids," called the storeman. He hooked his big thumbs under their arms. Up they swung. Lottie arranged the shawl "most beautifully", and the storeman tucked up their feet in a piece of old blanket.

"*Lift* up – Easy does it –" They might have been a couple of young ponies.

The storeman felt over the cords holding his load, unhooked the brake chain from the wheel, and whistling, he swung up beside them.

"Keep close to *me*," said Lottie, "because otherwise you pull the shawl away from my side, Kezia."

But Kezia edged up to the storeman – He towered up, big as a giant, and he smelled of nuts and wooden boxes.

# Chapter Two

It was the first time that Lottie and Kezia had ever been out so late. Everything looked different – the painted wooden houses much smaller than they did by day, the trees and the gardens far bigger and wilder. Bright stars speckled the sky and the moon hung over the harbour dabbling the waves with gold. They could see the light house shining from Quarantine Island, the green lights fore and aft on the old black coal hulks –

"There comes the Picton boat," said the storeman, pointing with his whip to a little steamer all hung with bright beads.

But when they reached the top of the hill and began to go down the other side, the harbour disappeared and although they were still in the town they were quite lost. Other carts rattled past. Everybody knew the storeman.

"Night, Fred!"

"Night-O!" he shouted.

Kezia liked very much to hear him. Whenever a cart appeared in the distance she looked up and waited for his voice. In fact she liked him altogether; he was an old friend; she and the grandmother had often been to his place to buy grapes. The storeman lived alone in a cottage with a glasshouse that he had built himself leaning against it. All the glasshouse was spanned and arched over with one beautiful vine. He took her brown basket from her, lined it with three large leaves and then he felt in his belt for a little horn knife, reached up and snipped off a big blue cluster and laid it on the leaves as tenderly as you might put a doll to bed. He was a very big man. He wore brown velvet trousers and he had a long brown beard, but he never wore a collar – not even on Sundays. The back of his neck was dark red.

"Where are we now?" Every few minutes one of the children asked him the question, and he was patient –
"Why! this is Hawstone Street," or "Hill Street" or "Charlotte Crescent" –
"Of course it is." Lottie pricked up her ears at the last name; she always felt that Charlotte Crescent belonged specially to her. Very few people had streets with the same name as theirs –
"Look, Kezia! There is Charlotte Crescent. Doesn't it look different."
They reached their last boundary marks – the fire alarm station – a little wooden affair painted red and sheltering a huge bell – and the white gates of the Botanical Gardens, gleaming in the moonlight. Now everything familiar was left behind; now the big dray rattled into unknown country, along the new roads with high clay banks on either side, up the steep, towering hills, down into valleys where the bush drew back on either side just enough to let them past, through a wide shallow river – the horses pulled up to drink – and made a rare scramble at starting again – on and on – further and further. Lottie drooped; her head wagged – she slipped half onto Kezia's lap and lay there. But Kezia could not open her eyes wide enough. The wind blew on them; she shivered but her cheeks and her ears burned. She looked up at the stars.
"Do stars ever blow about?" she asked.
"Well, I never *noticed* 'em," said the storeman.
Came a thin scatter of lights and the shape of a tin Church, rising out of a ring of tombstones.
"They call this place we're coming to – 'The Flats'," said the storeman.
"We got a nuncle and a naunt living near here," said Kezia –
"Aunt Doady and Uncle Dick. They've got two children, Pip,

the eldest is called and the youngest's name is Rags. He's got a
ram. He has to feed it with a nenamel teapot and a glove top over
the spout. He's going to show us. What is the difference between
a ram and a sheep."

"Well, a ram has got horns and it goes for you."

Kezia considered.

"I don't want to see it *frightfully*," she said. "I hate *rushing*
animals like dogs and parrots – don't you? I often dream that
animals rush at me – even camels, and while they're rushing,
their heads swell – e-normous!"

"My word!" said the storeman.

A very bright little place shone ahead of them and in front of
it was gathered a collection of traps and carts. As they drew near
some one ran out of the bright place and stood in the middle of
the road, waving his apron –

"Going to Mr Burnell's" shouted the some one.

"That's right," said Fred and drew rein.

"Well I got a passel for them in the store. Come inside half a
jiffy – will you?"

"We-ell! I got a couple of little kids along with me," said Fred.
But the some one had already darted back, across his verandah
and through the glass door. The storeman muttered something
about "stretching their legs" and swung off the dray.

"Where *are* we," said Lottie, raising up. The bright light from
the shop window shone over the little girls, Lottie's reefer cap
was all on one side and on her cheek there was the print of an
anchor button she had pressed against while sleeping. Tenderly
the storeman lifted her, set her cap straight and pulled down her
crumpled clothes. She stood, blinking on the verandah, watching
Kezia who seemed to come flying through the air to her feet. Into
the warm smoky shop they went – Kezia and Lottie sat on two
barrels, their legs dangling.

"Ma," shouted the man in the apron. He leaned over the
counter. "Name of Tubb!" he said, shaking hands with Fred.

"Ma!" he bawled. "Gotter couple of young ladies here." Came a wheeze from behind a curtain. "Arf a mo, dearie."

Everything was in that shop. Bluchers and sand shoes, straw hats and onions were strung across the ceiling, mixed with bunches of cans and tin teapots and broom heads and brushes. There were bins and canisters against the walls and shelves of pickles and jams and things in tins. One corner was fitted up as a drapers – you could smell the rolls of flannelette and one as a chemist's with cards of rubber dummies and jars of worm chocolate. One barrel brimmed with apples – one had a tap and a bowl under it half full of molasses, a third was stained deep red inside and a wooden ladle with a crimson handle was balanced across it. It held raspberries. And every spare inch of space was covered with a fly paper or an advertisement. Sitting on stools or boxes, or lounging against things a collection of big untidy men yarned and smoked. One, very old one with a dirty beard sat with his back half turned to the other, chewing tobacco and spitting a long distance into a huge round spitoon peppered with sawdust – After he had spat he combed his beard with a shaking hand. "We-ell! that's how it is!" or – "that's 'ow it 'appens" – or "there you've got it, yer see," he would quaver. But nobody paid any attention to him but Mr Tubb who cocked an occasional eye and roared "now, then Father" – And then the combing hand would be curved over the ear, and the silly face screw up – "Ay?" to droop again and again start chewing.

From the store the road completely changed – very slowly, twisting as if loath to go, turning as if shy to follow it slipped into a deep valley. In front and on either side there were paddocks and beyond them bush covered hills thrust up into the moonlit air were like dark heaving water – you could not imagine that the road led beyond the valley. Here it seemed to reach its perfect end – the valley knotted upon the bend of the road like a big jade tassel –

"Can we see the house from here the house from here" – piped the children. Houses were to be seen – little houses – they counted three – but not their house. The storeman knew – He had made the journey twice before that day – At last he raised his whip and pointed. "That's one of your paddocks belonging," he said "and the next and the next" – over the edge of the last paddock pushed tree boughs and bushes from an immense garden –

A corrugated iron fence painted white held back the garden from the road – In the middle there was a gap – the iron gates were open wide – They clanked through up a drive cutting through the garden like a whip lash, looping suddenly an island of green and behind the island out of sight until you came upon it was the house. It was long and low built with a pillared verandah and balcony running all the way round – shallow steps led to the door – The soft white bulk of it lay stretched upon the green garden like a sleeping beast – and now one and now another of the windows leaped into light – Some one was walking through the empty rooms carrying a lighted candle. From a window downstairs the light of a fire flickered – a strange beautiful excitement seemed to stream from the house in quivering ripples. Over its roofs, the verandah poles, the window sashes, the moon swung her lantern.

"Ooh" Kezia flung out her arms- The Grandmother had appeared on the top step – she carried a little lamp – she was smiling. "Has this house got a name" – asked Kezia fluttering for the last time out of the storeman's hands.

"Yes," said the Grandmother, "it is called Tarana." "Tarana" she repeated and put her hands upon the big glass door knob.

"Stay where you are one moment children." The Grandmother turned to the storeman. "Fred – these things can be unloaded and left on the verandah for the night. Pat will help you" – She turned and called into the hollow hall – "Pat are you there" – "I *am*" came a voice, and the Irish handy man squeaked in new boots over the bare boards. But Lottie staggered over the verandah like a bird fallen out of a nest – she stood still for a moment her eyes closed – if she leaned – she fell asleep. She could not walk another step – "Kezia" said the Grandmother "can I trust you to carry the lamp." "Yes, my Grandma" – The old woman knelt and gave the bright breathing thing into her hands and then she raised herself and caught up Lottie. "This way" – Through a square hall filled with furniture bales and hundreds of parrots (but the parrots were only on the wallpaper) down a narrow passage where the parrots persisted on either side walked Kezia with her lamp.

"You are to have some supper before you go to bed" said the Grandmother putting down Lottie to open the dining room door – "Be very quiet," she warned – "poor little mother has got such a headache."

Linda Burnell lay before a crackling fire in a long cane chair her feet on a hassock a plaid rug over her knees – Burnell and Beryl sat at a table in the middle of the room eating a dish of fried chops and drinking tea out of a brown china teapot – Over the back of her Mother's chair leaned Isabel – She had a white comb in her fingers and in a gentle absorbed way she was combing back the curls from her Mother's forehead – Outside the pool of lamp and firelight the room stretched dark and bare to the hollow windows – "Are those the children – " Mrs Burnell did not even open her eyes – her voice was tired and trembling – "Have either of them been maimed for life." "No dear – perfectly safe and sound."

"Put down that lamp Kezia," said Aunt Beryl "or we shall have the house on fire before we're out of the packing cases. More tea – Stan?" "Well you might just give me five-eighths of a cup," said Burnell, leaning across the table – "Have another chop Beryl – Tip top meat isn't it. First rate First rate. Not too lean – not too fat – " He turned to his wife – "Sure you won't change your mind – Linda darling?" "Oh the very thought of it" . . .

She raised one eyebrow in a way she had – The Grandmother brought the children two bowls of bread and milk and they sat up to the table, their faces flushed and sleepy behind the waving steam – "I had meat for my supper," said Isabel, still combing gently.

"I had a whole chop for my supper – the bone an' all, an Worcestershire sauce. Didn't I, Father – " "Oh, don't boast, Isabel," said Aunt Beryl. Isabel looked astounded – "I wasn't boasting was I mummy? I never thought of boasting – I thought they'd like to know. I only meant to tell them –" "Very well. That's enough" said Burnell. He pushed back his plate, took a tooth pick out of his waistcoat pocket and began picking his strong white teeth. "You might see that Fred has a bite of something in the kitchen before he goes, will you Mother." "Yes, Stanley." The old woman turned to go – "Oh and hold on a jiffy. I suppose nobody knows where my slippers were put. I suppose I shan't be able to get at 'em for a month or two eh?" "Yes," came from Linda. "In the top to the canvas hold all marked Urgent Necessities." "Well you might bring them to me will you Mother." "Yes Stanley." Burnell got up, stretched himself and went over to the fire to warm his bottom and lifted up his coat tail – "By Jove this is a pretty pickle, eh Beryl." Beryl sipping tea, her elbow on the table, smiled over the cup at him – She wore an unfamiliar pink pinafore. The sleeves of her blouse were rolled up to her shoulders showing her lovely freckled arms she had let her hair fall down her back in a long pig tail. "How long do you think it will take you to get straight – couple of weeks? eh –" he chaffed. "Good Heavens no," said Beryl. "The worst is over already. All the beds are up – Everything's in the house – yours and Linda's room is finished already. The servant girl and I have simply slaved all day and ever since Mother came she's worked like a horse, too. We've never sat down for a moment. We *have* had a day." Stamping he scented a rebuke. "Well I suppose you didn't expect me to tear away from the office and nail carpets

did you –" "Certainly not" said Beryl airily. She put dow.
cup and ran out of the dining room – "What the hell did s
expect to do," asked Stanley – "Sit down and fan herself with a
palm leaf fan while I hired a gang of professionals to do the job?
Eh? By Jove if she can't do a hand's turn occasionally without
shouting about it in return for —" and he glared as the chops
began to fight the tea in his sensitive stomach. But Linda put up
a hand and dragged him down – on to the side of her long cane
chair. "This is a wretched time for you old boy," she said
fondly – Her cheeks were very white but she smiled and curled
her fingers round the big red hand she held – "And with a wife
about as bright and gay as yesterday's button hole," she said –
"You've been awfully patient, darling." "Rot," said Burnell, but
he began to whistle the Holy City a good sign – "Think you're
going to like it?" he asked – "I don't want to tell you but I think
I ought to, Mother," said Isabel. "Kezia's drinking tea out of Aunt
Beryl's cup –"

They were trooped off to bed by the Grandmother – She went
first with a candle – the stairs rang to their climbing feet. Isabel
and Lottie lay in a room to themselves – Kezia curled in the
Grandmother's big bed. "Aren't there any sheets, my Grandma?"
"No, not to-night." "It's very tickly," said Kezia. "It's like Indians.
Come to bed soon an be my indian brave." "What a silly you are,"
said the old woman tucking her in as she loved to be tucked.
"Are you going to leave the candle." "No. Hush, go to sleep." "Well
kin I have the door left open?" She rolled herself into a round.
But she did not go to sleep. From All over the house came the
sound of steps – The house itself creaked and popped – Loud
whispery voices rose and fell. Once she heard Aunt Beryl's – rush
of high laughter. Once there came a loud trumpeting from
Burnell blowing his nose. Outside the windows hundreds of
black cats with yellow eyes sat in the sky watching her but she
was not frightened –

.tie was saying to Isabel – "I'm going to say my prayers in
.d to-night –" "No you can't Lottie." Isabel was very firm. "God
only excuses you saying your prayers in bed if you've got a
temperature." So Lottie yielded –

"Gentle Jesus meek an mile
Look 'pon little chile
Pity me simple Lizzie
Suffer me come to thee.
Fain would I to thee be brought
Dearest Lor' forbd it not
In the Kinkdom of thy grace
Make a little chile a place – Amen."

And then they lay down back to back their little behinds just
touching and fell asleep.

Standing in a pool of moonlight Beryl Fairfield undressed
herself – she was tired but she pretended to be more tired than
she really was – letting her clothes fall – pushing back with a
charming gesture her warm heavy hair – "Oh how tired I am
very tired" – she shut her eyes a moment but her lips smiled –
her breath rose and fell in her breast like fairy wings. The
window was open it was warm and still. Somewhere out there
in the garden a young man dark and slender with mocking eyes,
tip toed among the bushes and gathered the garden into a big
bouquet and slipped under her window and held it up to her –
She saw herself bending forward – He thrust his head among
the white waxy flowers – "No no," said Beryl. She turned from
the window she dropped her night gown over her head – "How
frightfully unreasonable Stanley is sometimes," she thought
buttoning – and then as she lay down came the old thought the
cruel leaping thought "if I had money" only to be shaken off
and beaten down by calling to her rescue her endless pack of
dreams – A young man immensely rich just arrived from

England meets her quite by chance. The new Governor is married. There is a ball at Government House to celebrate his wedding. Who is that exquisite creature in eau de nil satin Beryl Fairfield.

"The thing that pleases me" said Stanley leaning against the side of the bed in his shirt and giving himself a good scratch before turning in – "is that, on strict q.t. Linda I've got the place dirt cheap – I was talking about it to little Teddy Dean today and he said he simply couldn't understand why they'd accepted my figure you see land about here is bound to become more and more valuable – look in about ten years time . . . Of course we shall have to go very slow from now on and keep down expenses – cut 'em as fine as possible. Not asleep, are you." "No dear I'm listening –" said Linda. He sprang into bed leaned over her and blew out the candle. "Goodnight, Mr Business man" she said and she took hold of his head by the ears and gave him a quick kiss. Her faint far away voice seemed to come from a deep well – "Goodnight, darling." He slipped his arm under her neck and drew her to him . . . "Yes, clasp me," she said faintly, in her far away sleeping voice . . . .

Pat the handy man sprawled in his little room behind the kitchen. His sponge bag coat and trousers hung from the door peg like a hanged man. From the blanket edge his twisted feet protruded – and on the floor of his room there was an empty cane bird cage. He looked like a comic picture.

"Honk – honk" came from the snoring servant girl next door she had adenoids.

Last to go to bed was the Grandmother.

"What – not asleep yet." "No – I'm waiting for you," said Kezia. The old woman sighed and lay down beside her. Kezia thrust her head under the Grandmother's arm. "Who am I –" she whispered – this was an old established ritual to be gone through between them. "You are my little brown bird," said the Grandmother. Kezia gave a guilty chuckle. The Grandmother took out her teeth and put them in a glass of water beside her on the floor.

Then the house was still.

In the garden some tiny owls called – perched on the branches of a lace bark tree, More pork more pork, and far away from the bush came a harsh rapid chatter – Ha Ha Ha *Ha*. Ha-Ha-Ha-Ha!

Dawn came sharp and chill. The sleeping people turned over and hunched the blankets higher – They sighed and stirred but the brooding house all hung about with shadows held the quiet in its lap a little longer – A breeze blew over the tangled garden dropping dew and dropping petals – shivered over the drenched paddock grass lifted the sombre bush and shook from it a wild and bitter scent. In the green sky tiny stars floated a moment and then they were gone, they were dissolved like bubbles. The cocks shrilled from the neighbouring farms – the cattle moved in their stalls – the horses grouped under the trees lifted their heads and swished their tails – and plainly to be heard in the early quiet was the sound of the creek in the paddock running over the brown stones – running in and out of the sandy hollows – hiding under clumps of dark berry bushes – spilling into a swamp full of yellow water flowers and cresses – All the air smelled of water – The lawn was hung with bright drops and spangles – And then quite suddenly – at the first glint of sun – the birds began to sing – Big cheeky birds, starlings and minors whistled on the lawns; the little birds, the goldfinches and fantails and linnets twittered flitting from bough to bough – and from tree to tree, hanging the garden with bright chains of song – a lovely king fisher perched on the paddock fence preening his rich beauty – "How loud the birds are" said Linda in her dream. She was walking with her father through a green field sprinkled with daisies – and suddenly he bent forward and parted the grasses and showed her a tiny ball of fluff just at her feet. "Oh Papa the darling" She made a cup of her hands and caught the bird and stroked its head with her finger. It was quite tame. But a strange thing happened. As she stroked it it began to swell – It ruffled and pouched – it grew bigger and bigger and its round eyes seemed to smile at her – Now her arms were hardly wide enough to hold it – she dropped it in her apron. It had become a baby with a big naked head and a gaping bird mouth – opening and shutting – Her father broke into a loud clattering laugh and Linda woke to see Burnell standing by the windows rattling the Venetian blinds up to the very top – "Hullo" he said – "didn't wake you – did I? Nothing much the matter with the weather this morning." He was enormously pleased – weather like this set a final seal upon his bargain – he felt somehow – that he had bought the sun too got it chucked in, dirt cheap, with the house and grounds – He dashed off to his bath and Linda turned over, raised herself on one elbow to see the room by daylight. It looked wonderfully lived in already, all the furniture had found a place – all the old "paraphernalia" as she expressed it – even to photographs on the mantelpiece and medicine bottles on a shelf over the washstand. But this room was much bigger than their other room had been – that was a blessing. Her clothes lay across a chair – her outdoor things – a purple cape and a round sable with a plume on it – were tossed on the box ottoman – Looking at them a silly thought brought a fleeting smile into her eyes – "perhaps I am going away again to-day" and for a moment she saw herself driving away from them all in a little buggy – driving away from every one of them and waving – Back came Stanley girt with a towel, glowing and slapping his thighs. He pitched the wet towel on top of her cape and hat and standing firm in the exact centre of a square of sunlight he began to do his exercises – deep breathing – bending – squatting like a frog and shooting out his legs. He was so saturated with health that everything he did delighted him, but this amazing vigour seemed to set him miles and worlds away from Linda – she lay on the white tumbled bed, and leaned towards him laughing as if from the sky –

"Oh hang! Oh damn!" said Stanley who had butted into a crisp shirt only to find that some idiot had fastened the neck band and he was caught – He stalked over to her waving his arms. "Now you look the image of a fat turkey," said she – "Fat I like that" said Stanley – "why I haven't got a square inch of fat on me. Feel that – " "My dear – hard as nails" mocked she – "You'd be surprised – " said Stanley as though this were intensely interesting, "at the number of chaps in the club who've got a corporation – young chaps, you know – about my own age – " He began parting and brushing his strong ginger hair, his blue eyes fixed and round in the glass – bent at the knees because the dressing table was always – confound it – a bit too low for him. "Little Teddy Dean for example" and he straightened, describing upon himself an enormous curve with the hair brush. "Of course they're sitting on their hind quarters all day at the office and when they're away from it – as far as I can make out they stodge and they snooze – I must say I've got a perfect horror." "Yes my dear don't worry you'll never be fat – You're far too energetic," repeating the familiar formula that he never tired of hearing. "Yes. Yes I suppose that's true," and taking a mother of pearl pen knife out of his pocket he began to pare his nails – "Breakfast, Stanley" Beryl was at the door – "Oh Linda Mother says don't get up – Stay where you are until after lunch won't you?" She popped her head in at the door. She had a big piece of syringa stuck through a braid of her hair. "Everything we left on the verandah last night is simply sopping this morning. You should see poor dear Mother wringing out the sofa and chairs – however, no harm done – not a *pennorth's* of harm" this with the faintest glance at Stanley – "Have you told Pat what time to have the buggy round – It's a good six-and-a-half miles – from here to the office—" "I can imagine what his morning start off for the office will become" – thought Linda. Even when they lived in town – only half an hour away – the house had to slow down each morning – had to stop like a steamer – every soul on board summoned to the gangway to watch Burnell descending the ladder and into the little cockle shell – They must wave when he waved – give him good-bye for good-bye and lavish upon him unlimited loving sympathy as though they saw on the horizon's brim the untamed land to which he curved his chest so proudly, the line of leaping savages ready to fall upon his valiant sword –

"Pat Pat," she heard the servant girl calling – But Pat was evidently not to be found – the silly voice went baaing all over the garden. "It will be very high pressure indeed" – she decided – and did not rest again until the final slam of the front door sounded – and Stanley was gone.

Later she heard her children playing in the garden. Lottie's stolid compact little voice cried "Kezia Isabel" – Lottie was always getting lost or losing people and finding them again – astonished – round the next tree or the next corner – "Oh *there* you are" – They had been turned out to grass after breakfast with strict orders not to come near the house until they were called – Isabel wheeled a neat pram load of prim dolls and Lottie was allowed for a great treat to walk beside holding the doll parasols over the face of the wax one – "Where are you going Kezia," asked Isabel, who longed to find some light and menial duty that Kezia might perform and so be roped in under her government. "Oh just away," said Kezia.

"Come back, Kezia. Come back. You're not to go on the wet grass until it's dry. Grandma says," called Isabel.

"Bossy! bossy!" Linda heard Kezia answer.

"Do the children's voices annoy you, Linda," asked old Mrs Fairfield, coming in at that moment with a breakfast tray. "Shall I tell them to go further away from the house?"

"No, don't bother," said Linda. "Oh, Mother I do *not* want any breakfast."

"I have not brought you any," said Mrs Fairfield, putting down the tray on the bed table. "A spot of porridge, a finger of toast . . ."

"The merest sensation of marmalade – " mocked Linda – But

Mrs Fairfield remained serious. "Yes, dearie, and a little pot of fresh tea."

She brought from the cupboard a white woolen jacket trimmed with red bows and buttoned it round her daughter.

"Must I?" pouted Linda, making a face at the porridge.

Mrs Fairfield walked about the room. She lowered the blinds, tidied away the evidences of Burnell's toilet and gently she lifted the dampened plume of the little round hat. There was a charm and a grace in all her movements. It was not that she merely "set in order"; there seemed to be almost a positive quality in the obedience of things to her fine old hands. They found not only their proper but their perfect place. She wore a grey foulard dress patterned with white pansies, a white linen apron and one of those high caps shaped like a jelly mould of white tulle. At her throat a big silver brooch shaped like a crescent moon with five owls sitting on it and round her neck a black bead watch chain. If she had been a beauty in her youth and she had been a very great beauty – (Indeed, report had it that her miniature had been painted and sent to Queen Victoria as the belle of Australia) old age had touched her with exquisite gentleness. Her long curling hair was still black at her waist, grey between her shoulders and it framed her head in frosted silver. The late roses – the last roses – that frail pink kind, so reluctant to fall, such a wonder to find, still bloomed in her cheeks and behind big gold rimmed spectacles her blue eyes shone and smiled. And she still had dimples. On the backs of her hands, at her elbows – one in the left hand corner of her chin. Her body was the colour of old ivory. She bathed in cold water summer and winter and she could only bear linen next to her skin and suede gloves on her hands. Upon everything she used there lingered a trace of Cashmere bouquet perfume.

"How are you getting on downstairs," asked Linda, playing with her breakfast.

"Beautifully. Pat has turned out a treasure – He has laid all the linoleum and the carpets and Alice seems to be taking a *real interest* in the kitchen and pantries."

"Pantries! There's grandeur, after that bird cage of a larder in that other cubby hole!"

"Yes, I must say the house is wonderfully convenient and *ample* in every way. You should have a good look round when you get up."

Linda smiled, shaking her head.

"I don't want to. I don't *care*. The house can bulge cupboards and pantries, but other people will explore them. Not me."

"But *why* not," asked Mrs Fairfield, anxiously watching her.

"Because I don't feel the slightest crumb of interest, my Mother."

"But why don't you, dear? You ought to try – to begin – even for Stanley's sake. He'll be so bitterly disappointed if ... " Linda's laugh interrupted. "Oh, trust me – I'll satisfy Stanley. Besides I can *rave* all the better over what I haven't seen." "Nobody asks you to *rave*, Linda," said the old woman, sadly.

"Don't they?" Linda screwed up her eyes. "I'm not so sure. If I were to *jump* out of bed now, *fling* on my clothes, *rush* downstairs, *tear* up a ladder, hang pictures, eat an enormous lunch, romp with the children in the garden this afternoon and be swinging on the gate, waving, when Stanley hove in sight this evening I believe you'd be delighted – A normal, healthy day for a young wife and mother – A—"

Mrs Fairfield began to smile. "How absurd you are – How you exaggerate! What a baby you are," said she.

But Linda sat up suddenly and jerked off the "wooly".

"I'm boiling, I'm roasting," she declared. "I can't think what I'm doing in this big, stuffy old bed – I'm going to get up."

"Very well, dear," said Mrs Fairfield –

Getting dressed never took her long. Her hands flew. She had beautiful hands, white and tiny. The only *trouble* with them was that they would not keep her rings on them. Happily she only had two rings, her wedding ring and a peculiarly hideous affair, a square slab with four pin opals in it that Stanley had "stolen from a cracker" said Linda, the day they were engaged. But it was her wedding ring that disappeared so. It fell down every possible place and into every possible corner. Once she even found it in the crown of her hat. It was a familiar cry in the house "Linda's wedding ring has *gone again*" – Stanley Burnell could never hear that without a horrible sense of discomfort. Good Lord! he wasn't superstitious – He left that kind of rot to people who had nothing better to think about – but all the same, it was *devilishly* annoying. Especially as Linda made so light of the affair and mocked him and said "are they as expensive as all that" and laughed at him and cried, holding up her bare hand – "Look, Stanley, it has all been a dream." He was a fool to mind things like that, but they hurt him – they hurt like sin.

"Funny I should have dreamed about Papa last night" thought Linda, brushing her cropped hair that stood up all over her head in little bronzy rings. "What was it I dreamed?" No, she'd forgotten – "Something or other about a bird." But Papa was very plain – his lazy ambling walk. And she laid down the brush and went over to the marble mantelpiece and leaned her arms along it, her chin in her hands, and looked at his photograph. In his photograph he showed severe and imposing – a high brow, a piercing eye, clean shaven except for long "piccadilly weepers" draping his bosom. He was taken in the fashion of that time, standing, one arm on the back of a tapestry chair, the other clenched upon a parchment roll. "Papa!" said Linda, she smiled. "There you are my dear," she breathed, and then she shook her head quickly and frowned and went on with her dressing.

Her Father had died the year that she married Burnell, the year of her sixteenth birthday. All her childhood had been passed in a long white house perched on a hill overlooking Wellington harbour – a house with a wild garden full of bushes and fruit-trees, long, thick grass and nasturtiums. Nasturtiums grew everywhere – there was no fighting them down. They even fell in a shower over the paling fence on to the road. Red, yellow, white, every possible colour; they lighted the garden like swarms of butterflies. The Fairfields were a large family of boys and girls with their beautiful mother and their gay, fascinating father (for it was only in his photograph that he looked stern) they were quite a "show" family and immensely admired. Mr Fairfield managed a small insurance business that could not have been very profitable, yet they lived plentifully. He had a good voice; he liked to sing in public, he liked to dance and attend picnics – to put on his "bell topper" and walk out of Church if he disapproved of anything said in the sermon – and he had a passion for inventing highly unpracticable things, like collapsible umbrellas or folding lamps. He had one saying with which he met all difficulties. "Depend upon it, it will all come right after the Maori war." Linda, his second to youngest child, was his darling, his pet, his playfellow. She was a wild thing, always trembling on the verge of laughter, ready for anything and eager. When he put his arm round her and held her he felt her thrilling with life. He understood her so beautifully and gave her so much love for love that he became a kind of daily miracle to her and all her faith centred in him – People barely touched her; she was regarded as a cold, heartless little creature, but she seemed to have an unlimited passion for that violent sweet thing called life – just being alive and able to run and climb and swim in the sea and lie in the grass. In the evenings she and her Father would sit on the verandah – she on his knees – and "plan". "When I am grown up we shall travel everywhere – we shall see the whole world – won't we Papa?"

"We shall, my dear."

"One of your inventions will have been a great success – Bring you in a good round million yearly."

"We can manage on that."

"But one day we shall be rich and the next poor. One day we

shall dine in a palace and the next we'll sit in a forest and toast mushrooms on a hatpin ... We shall have a little boat – we shall explore the interior of China on a raft – you will look sweet in one of those huge umbrella hats that Chinamen wear in pictures. We won't leave a corner of anywhere unexplored – shall we?"

"We shall look under the beds and in all the cupboards and behind every curtain."

"And we shan't go as father and daughter," she tugged at his "piccadilly weepers" and began kissing him. "We'll just go as a couple of boys together – Papa."

By the time Linda was fourteen the big family had vanished, only she and Beryl, who was two years younger, were left. The girls had married; the boys had gone faraway – Linda left off attending the Select Academy for Young Ladies presided over by Miss Clara Finetta Birch (From England) a lady whose black hair lay so flat on her head that *everybody said* it was only painted on, and she stayed at home to be a help to her mother. For three days she laid the table and took the mending basket on to the verandah in the afternoon but after that she "went mad-dog again" as her father expressed it and there was no holding her. "Oh, Mother, life is so *fearfully short*," said Linda. That summer Burnell appeared. Every evening a stout young man in a striped shirt, with fiery red hair and a pair of immature mutton chop whiskers passed their house, quite slowly, four times. Twice up the hill he went and twice down he came. He walked with his hands behind his back and each time he glanced once at the verandah where they sat – Who was he? None of them knew, but he became a great joke. "Here she blows," Mr Fairfield would whisper. The young man came to be called the "Ginger Whale" – Then he appeared at Church, in a pew facing theirs, very devout and serious. But he had that unfortunate complexion that goes with his colouring and every time he so much as glanced in Linda's direction a crimson flush spread over his face to his ears. "Look out, my wench," said Mr Fairfield. "Your clever Papa has solved the problem. That young fellow is after you."

"Henry! What rubbish. How can you say such things," said his wife.

"There are times," said Linda, "when I simply doubt your *sanity* Papa." But Beryl loved the idea. The ginger whale became "Linda's beau".

"You know as well I do that I am *never* going to marry," said Linda. "How can you be such a *traitor,* Papa – "

A social given by the Liberal Ladies Political League ripened matters a little. Linda and her Papa attended. She wore a green sprigged muslin with little capes on the shoulders that stood up like wings and he wore a frock coat and a wired buttonhole as big as a soup plate. The social began with a very "painful" concert. "She wore a wreath of roses" – "They played in the Beautiful Garden" "A Mother sat Watching" – "Flee Like a Bird to the Fountain" sang the political ladies with forlorn and awful vigour – The gentlemen sang with far greater vigour and a kind of defiant cheerfulness which was almost terrifying. They looked very furious, too. Their cuffs shot over their hands, or their trousers were far too long . . . Comic recitations about flies on bald heads and engaged couples sitting on porch steps spread with glue were contributed by the chemist. Followed an extraordinary meal called upon the hand printed programme Tea and Coffee and consisting of ham-beef-or-tongue, tinned salmon oyster patties, sanwiches, col' meat, jellies, huge cakes, fruit salad in wash hand bowls, trifles bristling with almonds and large cups of tea, dark brown in colour, tasting faintly of rust. Helping Linda to a horrible-looking pink blanc-mange which Mr Fairfield said was made of strangled baby's head, he whispered – "the ginger whale is here. I've just spotted him blushing at a sanwich. Look out, my lass. He'll sandbag you with one of old Ma Warren's rock cakes." Away went the plates – away went the table. Young Mr Fantail, in evening clothes with brown button boots sat down at the piano – and crashed into the "Lancers".

Diddle dee dum tee tum te tum

Diddle dee um te tum te tum

. . .

Diddle dee tum tee diddle tee tum!

And half way through the "evening" it actually came to pass – Smoothing his cotton gloves, a beetroot was *pale* compared to him a pillar box was a tender pink. Burnell asked Linda for the pleasure and before she realised what had happened his arm was round her waist and they were turning round and round to the air of "Three Blind Mice" (arranged by Mr Fantail même). He did not talk while he danced, but Linda liked that. She felt a "silly" – When the dance was over they sat on a bench against the wall. Linda hummed the waltz tune and beat time with her glove – She felt dreadfully shy and she was terrified of her father's merry eye – At last Burnell turned to her. "Did you ever hear the story of the shy young man who went to his first ball. He danced with a girl and then they sat on the stairs – and they could not think of a thing to say – And after he'd picked up everything she dropped from time to time – after the silence was simply unbearable he turned round and stammered 'd-do you always w-wear fl-f-flannel next to the skin?' I feel rather like that chap," said Burnell.

Then she did not hear them anymore. What a glare there was in the room. She hated blinds pulled up to the top at any time – but in the morning, in the morning especially! She turned over to the wall and idly, with one finger, she traced a poppy on the wallpaper with a leaf and a stem and a fat bursting bud. In the quiet, under her tracing finger, the poppy seemed to come alive. She could feel the sticky, silky petals, the stem, hairy like a gooseberry skin, the rough leaf and the tight glazed bud. Things had a habit of coming alive in the quiet; she had often noticed it. Not only large, substantial things, like furniture, but curtains and the patterns of stuffs and fringes of quilts and cushions. How often she had seen the tassel fringe of her quilt change into a funny procession of dancers, with priests attending . . . For there *were* some tassels that did not dance at all but walked stately, bent forward as if praying or chanting. . . How often the medicine bottles had turned into a row of little men with brown top hats on; and often the wash stand jug sat in the basin like a fat bird in a round nest "I dreamed about birds last night" thought Linda. What was it? No, she'd forgotten . . . But the strangest part about this coming alive of things was what they did. They listened; they seemed to swell out with some mysterious important content and when they were full she felt that they smiled – Not for her (although she knew they "recognised" her) their sly meaning smile; they were members of a secret order and they smiled among themselves. Sometimes, when she had fallen asleep in the day time, she woke and could not lift a finger, could not even turn her eyes to left or right . . . *they* were so strong; sometimes when she went out of a room and left it empty she knew as she clicked the door to that *they* were coming to life. And Ah, there were times, especially in the evenings when she was upstairs, perhaps, and everybody else was down when she could hardly tear herself away from "them" – when she could not hurry, when she tried to hum a tune to show them she did not care, when she tried to say ever so carelessly – "Bother that old thimble! Where ever have I put it!" but she never never deceived *them. They* knew how frightened she was; "they" saw how she turned her head away as she passed the mirror. For all their patience they wanted something of her. Half unconsciously she knew that if she gave herself up and was quiet – more than quiet, silent, motionless, something would happen . . . "It's very very quiet now," thought Linda. She opened her eyes wide; she heard the stillness spinning its soft endless web. How lightly she breathed – She scarcely had to breathe at all . . . Yes, everything had come alive down to the minutest, tiniest particle and she did not feel her bed – She floated, held up in the air. Only she seemed to be listening with her wide open watchful eyes, waiting for someone to come who just did not come, watching for something to happen that just did not happen.

In the kitchen at the long deal table under the two windows old Mrs Fairfield was washing the breakfast dishes. The kitchen windows looked out on to a big grass patch that led down to the vegetable garden and the rhubarb beds – On one side the grass patch was bordered by the scullery and wash house and over this long white washed "lean to" there grew a big knotted vine. She had noticed yesterday that some tiny corkscrew tendrils had come right through some cracks in the scullery ceiling and all the windows of the "lean to" had a thick frill of dancing green. "I am very fond of a grape vine," decided Mrs Fairfield, "but I do not think that the grapes will ripen here. It takes Australian sun ..." and she suddenly remembered how when Beryl was a baby she had been picking some white grapes from the vine on the back verandah of their Tasmanian house and she had been stung on the leg by a huge red ant. She saw Beryl in a little plaid dress with red ribbon "tie ups" on the shoulders screaming so dreadfully that half the street had rushed in ... and the child's leg had swelled to an enormous size ... "T-t-t-t" Mrs Fairfield caught her breath, remembering. "Poor child – how terrifying it was!" and she set her lips tight in a way she had and went over to the stove for some more hot water – The water frothed up in the big soapy bowl with pink and blue bubbles on top of the foam. Old Mrs Fairfield's arms were bare to the elbow and stained a bright pink. She wore a grey foulard dress patterned with large purple pansies, a white linen apron and a high cap shaped like a jelly mould of white tulle. At her throat there was a silver crescent moon with five little owls seated on it and round her neck she wore a watch guard made of black beads. It was very hard to believe that they had only arrived yesterday and that she had not been in the kitchen for years – she was so much a part of it, putting away the clean crocks with so sure and precise a touch, moving, leisurely and ample from the stove to the dresser, looking into the pantry and the larder as though there were not an unfamiliar corner. When she had finished tidying everything in the kitchen had become part of a series of pattern. She stood in the middle of the room, wiping her hands on a check towel and looking about her, a tiny smile beamed on her lips; she thought it looked very nice, very satisfactory. If only servant girls could be taught to understand that it did not only matter how you put a thing away it mattered just as much *where* you put it – or was it the other way about... But at any rate they never would understand; she had never been able to train them ... "Mother, Mother are you in the kitchen?" called Beryl. "Yes, dear. Do you want me?" "No, I'm coming," and Beryl ran in, very flushed, dragging with her two big pictures. "Mother whatever can I do with these hideous awful Chinese paintings that Chung Wah gave Stanley when he went bankrupt. It's absurd to say they were valuable because they were hanging in Chung Wah's fruit shop for months before. I can't understand why Stanley doesn't want them to be thrown away – I'm sure he thinks they're just as hideous as we do, but it's because of the frames – " she said, spitefully. "I suppose he thinks the frames might fetch something one day. Ugh! What a weight they are." "Why don't you hang them in the passage" suggested Mrs Fairfield. "They would not be much seen there." "I can't. There isn't room. I've hung all the photographs of his office before and after rebuilding there, and the signed photographs of his business friends and that awful enlargement of Isabel lying on a mat in her singlet. There isn't an inch of room left there." Her angry glance flew over the placid kitchen. "I know what I'll do. I'll hang them here – I'll say they got a little damp in the moving and so I put them up here in the warm for the time being." She dragged forward a chair, jumped up on it, took a hammer and a nail out of her deep apron pocket and banged away – "There! That's high enough.

Hand me up the picture, Mother." "One moment, child – " she was wiping the carved ebony frame – "Oh, Mother, *really* you need not dust them. It would take years to dust all those winding little holes" and she frowned at the top of her Mother's head and bit her lip with impatience. Mother's deliberate way of doing things was simply maddening. It was old age, she supposed, loftily. At last the two pictures were hung, side by side. She jumped off the chair, stowing back the little hammer. "They don't look so bad there, do they," said she – "And at any rate nobody need ever see them except Pat and the servant girl – Have I got a spider's web on my face, Mother? I've been poking my head into that cupboard under the stairs and now something keeps tickling me." But before Mrs Fairfield had time to look Beryl had turned away again – "Is that clock right. Is it really as early as that? Good Heavens it seems years since breakfast?" "That reminds me," said Mrs Fairfield. "I must go upstairs and fetch down Linda's tray" . . . "There!" cried Beryl. "Isn't that like the servant girl. Isn't that exactly like her. I told her distinctly to tell you that I was too busy to take it up and would you please instead. I never dreamed she hadn't told you!"

Some one tapped on the window. They turned away from the pictures. Linda was there, nodding and smiling. They heard the latch of the scullery door lift and she came in. She had no hat on; her hair stood up on her head in curling rings and she was all wrapped up in an old Kashmir shawl. "Please can I have something to eat," said she. "Linnet dear I am so frightfully sorry. It's my fault," cried Beryl. "But I wasn't hungry. I would have screamed if I had been," said Linda "Mummy darling, make me a little pot of tea in the brown china teapot." She went into the pantry and began lifting the lids off a row of tins. "What grandeur my dears," she cried, coming back with a brown scone and a slice of gingerbread – "a pantry and a larder." "Oh but you haven't seen the outhouses yet" said Beryl. "There is a stable and a huge barn of a place that Pat calls the feed room and a woodshed and a tool house – all built round a square courtyard that has big white gates to it. Awfully grand!" "This is the first time I've even seen the kitchen" said Linda. "Mother has been here. Everything is in pairs." "Sit down and drink your tea," said Mrs Fairfield, spreading a clean table napkin over a corner of the table. "And Beryl have a cup with her. I'll watch you both while I'm peeling the potatoes for dinner. I don't know what has happened to the servant girl." "I saw her on my way downstairs, Mummy. She's lying practically at full length on the bathroom floor laying linoleum. And she is hammering it so frightfully hard that I am sure the pattern will come through on to the dining-room ceiling. I told her not to run any more tacks than she could help into herself but I am afraid that she will be studded for life all the same. Have half my piece of gingerbread, Beryl. Beryl, do you like the house now that we are *here*?" "Oh yes I like the house immensely and the garden is simply beautiful but it feels very far away from everything to me. I can't imagine people coming out from town to see us in that dreadful rattling' bus and I am sure there isn't anybody here who will come and call . . . Of course it doesn't matter to you particularly because you never liked living in town." "But we've got the buggy," said Linda. "Pat can drive you into town whenever you like. And after all it's only six miles away." That was a consolation certainly but there was something unspoken at the back of Beryl's mind, something she did not even put into words for herself. "Oh, well at any rate it won't kill us," she said dryly, putting down her cup and standing up and stretching. "I am going to hang curtains." And she ran away singing: "How many thousand birds I see, That sing aloft in every tree." But when she reached the dining room she stopped singing. Her face changed – hardened, became gloomy and sullen. "One may as well rot here as anywhere else," she said savagely digging the stiff brass safety pins into the red serge curtains . . .

The two left in the kitchen were quiet for a little. Linda leaned her cheek in her fingers and watched her Mother. She thought her Mother looked wonderfully beautiful standing with her back to the leafy window – There was something comforting in the sight of her Mother that Linda felt she could never do without – She knew everything about her – just what she kept in her pocket and the sweet smell of her flesh and the soft feel of her cheeks and her arms and shoulders, still softer – the way the breath rose and fell in her bosom and the way her hair curled silver round her forehead, lighter at her neck and bright brown still in the big coil under the tulle cap. Exquisite were her Mother's hands and the colour of the two rings she wore seemed to melt into her warm white skin – her wedding ring and a large old fashioned ring with a dark red stone in it that had belonged to Linda's father . . . And she was always so fresh so delicious. "Mother, you smell of cold water," she had said – The old woman could bear nothing next to her skin but fine linen and she bathed in cold water summer and winter – even when she had to pour a kettle of boiling water over the frozen tap. "Isn't there anything for me to do, Mother," she asked. "No darling. Run and see what the garden is like. I wish you would give an eye to the children but that I know you will not do." "Of course I will, but you know Isabel is much more grown up than any of us." "Yes, but Kezia is not" said Mrs Fairfield. "Oh Kezia's been tossed by a wild bull *hours* ago" said Linda, winding herself up in her shawl again.

But no, Kezia had seen a bull through a hole in a notch of wood in the high paling fence that separated the tennis lawn from the paddock, but she had not liked the bull frightfully and so she had walked away back through the orchard up the grassy slope along the path by the lace bark tree and so into the spread tangled garden. She did not believe that she would ever not get lost in this garden. Twice she had found her way to the big iron gates they had driven through last night and she had begun to walk up the drive that led to the house, but there were so many little paths on either side — on one side they all led into a tangle of tall dark trees and strange bushes with flat velvety leaves and feathery cream flowers that buzzed with flies when you shook them – this was a frightening side and no garden at all. The little paths were wet and clayey with tree roots spanned across them, "like big fowls feet" thought Kezia. But on the other side of the drive there was a high box border and the paths had box edgings and all of them led into a deeper and deeper tangle of flowers. It was summer. The camellia trees were in flower, white and crimson and pink and white striped with flashing leaves – you could not see a leaf on the syringa bushes for the white clusters. All kinds of roses – gentlemen's button hole roses, little white ones but far too full of insects to put under anybody's nose, pink monthly roses with a ring of fallen petals round the bushes, cabbage roses on thick fat stalks, moss roses, always in bud, pink smooth beauties opening curl on curl, red ones so dark that they seemed to turn black as they fell and a certain exquisite cream kind with a slender red stem and bright red leaves. Kezia knew the name of that kind: it was her grandmother's favourite. There were clumps of fairy bells and cherry pie and all kinds of geraniums and there were little trees of verbena and bluish lavender bushes and a bed of pelagoniums with velvet eyes and leaves like moth's wings. There was a bed of nothing but mignonette and another of nothing but pansies – borders of double and single daisies, all kinds of little tufty plants.

The red hot pokers were taller than she; the Japanese sunflowers grew in a tiny jungle. She sat down on one of the box borders. By pressing hard at first it made a very pleasant springy seat but how dusty it was inside – She bent down to look and sneezed and rubbed her nose. And then she found herself again at the top of the rolling grassy slope that led down to the orchard and beyond the orchard to an avenue of pine trees with wooden seats between bordering one side of the tennis court. .

. She looked at the slope a moment; then she lay down on her back gave a tiny squeak and rolled over and over into the thick flowery orchard grass. As she lay still waiting for things to stop spinning round she decided to go up to the house and ask the servant girl for an empty match-box. She wanted to make a surprise for the grandmother. First she would put a leaf inside with a big violet lying on it – then she would put a very small little white picotee perhaps, on each side of the violet and then she would sprinkle some lavender on the top, but not to cover their heads. She often made these surprises for the grandmother and they were always most successful: "Do you want a match, my Granny?" "Why, yes, child. I believe a match is the very thing I am looking for –" The Grandmother slowly opened the box and came upon the picture inside. "Good gracious child! how you astonished me!" "Did I – did I really astonish you?" Kezia threw up her arms with joy. "I can make her one every day here" she thought, scrambling up the grass slope on her slippery shoes. But on her way to the house she came to the island that lay in the middle of the drive, dividing the drive into two arms that met in front of the house. The island was made of grass banked up high. Nothing grew on the green top at all except one round plant with thick grey-green thorny leaves and out of the middle there sprang up a tall stout stem. Some of the leaves of this plant were so old that they curved up in the air no longer, they turned back – they were split and broken – some of them lay flat and withered on the ground – but the fresh leaves curved up in to the air with their spiked edges; some of them looked as though they had been painted with broad bands of yellow. Whatever could it be? She had never seen anything like it before – She stood and stared. And then she saw her Mother coming down the path with a red carnation in her hand – "Mother what is it?" asked Kezia. Linda looked up at the fat swelling plant with its cruel leaves its towering fleshy stem. High above them, as though becalmed in the air, and yet holding so fast to the earth it grew from it might have had claws and not roots. The curving leaves seemed to be hiding something; the big blind stem cut into the air as if no wind could ever shake it. "That is an aloe, Kezia," said Linda. "Does it ever have any flowers." "Yes my child" said her Mother and she smiled down at Kezia, half shutting her eyes, "once every hundred years."

# Chapter Three

On his way home from the office Stanley Burnell stopped the buggy at the "Bodega", got out and bought a large bottle of oysters. At the chinaman's shop next door he bought a pineapple in the pink of condition and noticing a basket of fresh black cherries he told John to put him up a pound of those as well. The oysters and pineapple he stowed away in the box under the front seat – but the cherries he kept in his hand. Pat, the handy man, leapt off the box and tucked him up again in a brown rug. "Lift yer feet, Mr Burnell while I give her a fold under," said he. "Right, right – first rate!" said Stanley – "you can make straight for home now." "I believe this man is a first rate chap" thought he as Pat gave the grey mare a touch and the buggy sprang forward. He liked the look of him sitting up there in his neat dark brown coat and brown bowler – he liked the way Pat had tucked him in and he liked his eyes – There was nothing servile about him, – and if there was one thing he hated more than another in a servant it was servility – and he looked as though he were pleased with his job – happy and contented. The grey mare went very well. Burnell was impatient to be out of the town. He wanted to be home. Ah, it was splendid to live in the country – to get right out of this hole of a town once the office was closed and this long drive in the fresh warm air knowing all the time that his own house was at the other end with its garden and paddocks, its three tip top cows and enough fowls and ducks to keep them in eggs and poultry was splendid, too. As they left the town finally and bowled away up the quiet road his heart beat hard for joy – He rooted in the bag and began to eat the cherries, three or four at a time chucking the stones over the side of the buggy. They were delicious, so plump and cold without a spot or a bruise on them. Look at these two now – black one side and white the other – perfect – a perfect little pair of Siamese twins – and he stuck them in his button hole – By Jove, he wouldn't mind giving that chap up there a handful, but no, better not! Better wait until he had been with him a bit longer. He began to plan what he would do with his Saturday afternoons and Sundays. He wouldn't go to the Club for lunch on Saturday. No, cut away from the office as soon as possible and get them to give him a couple of slices of cold meat and half a lettuce when he got home. And then he'd get a few chaps out from town to play tennis in the afternoons. Not too many – three at most. Beryl was a good player too. He stretched out his right arm and slowly bent it, feeling the muscles. A bath, a good rub down, a cigar on the verandah after dinner. On Sunday morning they would go to church – children and all – which reminded him that he must hire a pew in the sun if possible – and well forward so as to be out of the draught from the door – In fancy he heard himself intoning, extremely well:

"When-thou-didst-overcome the sharpness of death Thou didst open the *King*dom of Heaven to *All* Believers" and he saw the neat brass edged card on the corner of the pew "Mr Stanley Burnell and Family." The rest of the day he'd loaf about with Linda. Now she was on his arm; they were walking about the garden together and he was explaining to her at length what he intended doing at the office the week following. He heard her saying: "My dear, I think that is *most* wise." Talking things out with Linda was a wonderful help even though they were apt to drift away from the point . . . Hang it all! They weren't getting along very fast. Pat had put the brake on again. "He's a bit too ready with that brake! Ugh! What a brute of a thing it is – I can feel it in the pit of my stomach." A sort of panic overtook Burnell whenever he approached near home. Before he was well inside the gate he would shout to any one in sight, "is everything all right?" and then he did not believe it was until he heard Linda cry "Hullo, you old boy!" That was the worst of living in the country. It took the deuce of a long time to get back. But now they weren't far off. They were on top of the last hill – it was a gentle slope all the way now and not more than half a mile. Pat kept up a constant trailing of the whip across the mare's back and he coaxed her – "goop now goop now!" It wanted a few moments to sunset, everything stood motionless bathed in bright metallic light and from the paddocks on either side there streamed the warm milky smell of ripe hay – The iron gates were open. They dashed through and up the drive and round the island stopping at the exact middle of the verandah. "Did she satisfy yer, sir," said Pat, getting off the box and grinning at his master. "Very well indeed Pat," said Stanley. Linda came out of the glass door – out of the shadowy hall – her voice rang in the quiet. "Hullo, you're home again." At the sound of it his happiness beat up so hard and strong that he could hardly stop himself dashing up the steps and catching her in his arms – "Yes home again. Is everything all right." "Perfect" said she. Pat began to lead the mare round to the side gate that gave onto the courtyard. "Here half a moment" said Burnell "Hand me those two parcels – will you." And he said to Linda "I've brought you back a bottle of oysters and a pineapple" as though he had brought her back all the harvest of the earth. They went into the hall; Linda carried the oysters under one arm and the pineapple under the other – Burnell shut the glass door threw his hat on the hall stand and put his arms round her, straining her to him kissing the top of her head, her ears her lips – her eyes – "Oh dear Oh dear" she said "Wait a minute let me put down these *silly* things" and she put down the bottle of oysters and the pine on a little carved chair – "What have you got in your buttonhole, cherries?" – and she took them out and hung them over his ear. "No don't do that darling. They're for you." So she took them off his ear and ran them through her brooch pin – "You don't mind if I don't eat them now. Do you? They'll spoil my appetite for dinner – Come and see your children. They're having tea." The lamp was lighted on the nursery table: Mrs Fairfield was cutting and spreading bread and butter and the three little girls sat up to table wearing large bibs embroidered with their names. They wiped their mouths as their Father came in ready to be kissed. There was jam on the table too a plate of home made knobbly buns and cocoa steaming in a Dewar's Whisky Advertisement jug – a big toby jug, half brown half cream with a picture of a man on it smoking a long clay pipe. The windows were wide open. There was a jar of wild flowers on the mantelpiece and the lamp made a big soft bubble of light on the ceiling – "You seem pretty snug Mother" said Burnell, looking round and blinking at the light and smiling at the little girls. They sat Isabel and Lottie on either side of the table, Kezia at the bottom – the place at the top was empty – "That's where my boy ought to sit" thought Stanley – He tightened his arm round Linda's shoulder. By God! he was a perfect fool to feel as happy as this— "We are Stanley. We are very snug," said Mrs Fairfield, cutting Kezia's bread and jam into fingers. "Like it better than town eh children" said Burnell. "Oh yes, Daddy" said the three little girls and Isabel added as an afterthought, "Thank you very much *indeed* Father dear."

"Come upstairs and have a wash" said Linda – "I'll bring your slippers." But the stairs were too narrow for them to go up arm in arm. It was quite dark in their room – He heard her ring tapping the marble as she felt along the mantelpiece for matches. "I've got some darling. I'll light the candles." But instead, he came up behind her and caught her put his arms round her and pressed her head into his shoulder. "I'm so confoundedly happy" he said. "Are you?" She turned and put her two hands flat on his breast and looked up at him – "I don't know what's come

over me" he protested. It was quite dark outside now and heavy
dew was falling. When she shut the window the dew wet her
finger tips. Far away, a dog barked. "I believe there's going to be
a moon" said she – At the words and with the wet cold dew
touching her lips and cheeks she felt as though the moon had
risen – that she was being bathed in cold light – she shivered she
came away from the window and sat down on the box ottoman
beside Stanley –

In the dining room by the flickering glow of a wood fire Beryl
sat on a hassock playing the guitar. She had bathed and changed
all her clothes. Now she wore a white muslin dress with big black
spots on it and in her hair she had pinned a black rose –

Nature has gone to her rest love
See we are all alone
Give me your hand to press love
Lightly within my own –

She played and sang half to herself – for she was watching herself
playing and singing she saw the fire light on her shoes and skirt
on the ruddy belly of the guitar on her white fingers. "If I were
outside the window and looked in and saw myself I really would
be rather struck" she thought – Still more softly she played the
accompaniment not singing – "The first time I ever saw you little
girl you had no idea that you weren't alone! You were sitting with
your little feet up on a hassock playing the guitar – I can never
forget – " and she flung back her head at the imaginary speaker
and began to sing again

Even the moon is aweary –

But there came a loud knock at the door. The servant girl popped
in her flushed face. "If you please Miss – kin I come and lay the
dinner" – "Certainly Alice" said Beryl – in a voice of ice. She put

the guitar in a corner – Alice lunged in with a heavy black iron tray, "Well I *ave* had a job with that oving" said she. "I can't get nothing to brown."

*"Really"* said Beryl – But no, she could not bear that fool of a girl – She went into the dark drawing room and began walking up and down – She was restless, restless restless. There was a mirror over the mantelpiece she leaned her arms along and looked at her pale shadow in it – "I look as though I have been drowned" – said she –

# Chapter Four

## Children and Ducks

"Good Morning Mrs Jones." "Oh, good morning Mrs Smith. I'm so glad to see you. Have you brought your children?" "Yes, I've brought both my twins. I have had another baby since I saw you last but she came so suddenly that I haven't had time to make her any clothes yet and so I left her at home. How's your husband." "Oh he's very well thank you. At least he had an awful sore throat, but Queen Victoria (she's my grandmother you know) sent him a case of pineapples and they cured it immediately – Is that your new servant." "Yes, her name's Gwen. I've only had her two days – Oh Gwen, this is my friend Mrs Smith." "Good morning Mrs Smith. Dinner won't not be ready for about ten minutes." "I don't think you ought to introduce me to the servant, I think I ought to just begin talking to her." "Well she isn't really quite a servant. She's more of a lady help than a servant and you do introduce Lady Helps I know because Mrs Samuel Josephs had one." "Oh well, it doesn't *matter*" said the new servant airily, beating up a chocolate custard with half a broken clothes peg. The dinner was baking beautifully on a concrete step – She began to lay the cloth on a broad pink garden seat. In front of each person she put two geranium leaf plates, a pine needle fork and a twig knife. There were three daisy heads on a laurel leaf for poached eggs, some slices of fuchsia petals for cold meat, some beautiful little rissoles made of earth and water and dandelion seeds, and the chocolate custard. Which she decided to serve in the pawa shell she had cooked it in – "You needn't trouble about my children" said Mrs Smith graciously – "If you'll just take this bottil and fill it at the tap – I mean in the dairy." "Oh all right" said Gwen and she whispered to Mrs Jones "Shall I go an ask Alice for a little bit of real milk?" But some one called from the front of the house "children children" and the luncheon party melted away leaving the charming table leaving the rissoles and the eggs on the stove – to the little ants and to an old snail who pushed his quivering horns over the edge of the pink garden seat and began slowly to nibble a geranium plate. "Come round to the front door children. Rags and Pip have come." The Trout Boys were cousins to the Burnells. They lived about a mile away in a house called Monkey Tree Cottage. Pip was tall for his age with lank black hair and a white face but Rags was very small, and so thin that when he was undressed his shoulder blades stuck out like two little wings. They had a mongrel dog too with pale blue eyes and a long tail that turned up at the end who followed them everywhere; he was called Snooker. They were always combing and brushing Snooker and treating him in various extraordinary mixtures concocted by Pip and kept secredy by him in a broken jug to be diluted in a kerosene tin of hot water and applied to the shivering creature but Snooker was always full of fleas and he stank abominably.

He would see Pip mix some carbolic tooth powder and a bit of sulphur powdered fine and perhaps a pinch of starch to stiffen up Snooker's coat but he knew that was not all. There was something else added that Pip wouldn't tell him of covered with an old kettle lid. Rags privately thought it was gunpowder. Even Rags was not allowed to share the secret of these mixtures. And he was never never on any account permitted to help or to look on because of the danger – "Why if a spot of this flew up" Pip would say, stirring the mixture with an iron spoon "you'd be blinded to death and there's always the chance – just the chance of it exploding – if you whack it hard enough. Two spoon fulls of this will be enough in a kerosene tin of water to kill thousands of fleas." Nevertheless Snooker spent all his leisure biting and nudging himself and he stank abominably – "It's because he's such a grand fighting dog" Pip would say. "All fighting dogs smell –" The Trout boys had often gone into town and spent the day with the Burnells but now that they had become neighbours and lived in this big house and bonzer garden they were inclined to be very friendly. Besides both of them liked playing with girls – Pip because he could fox them so and because Lottie Burnell was so easily frightened and Rags for a shameful reason because he adored dolls. The way he would look at a doll as it lay asleep, speaking in a whisper and smiling timidly and the great treat it was to him to stretch out his arms and be given a doll to hold! "Curl your arms round her. Don't keep them stiff out like that. You'll drop her" Isabel would command sternly.

Now they were standing on the verandah and holding back Snooker who wanted to go into the house but wasn't allowed to because Aunt Linda hated decent dogs. "We came over on the bus with Mum," they said "and we're going to spend the afternoon and stay to tea. We brought over a batch of our gingerbread for Aunt Linda. Our Minnie made it. It's all over nuts – much more than yours ever has." "I shelled the almonds" said Pip. "I just stuck my hand in a saucepan of boiling water and grabbed them out and gave them a kind of pinch and the nuts flew out of the shells some of them as high as the ceiling. Didn't they Rags?" "When they make cakes at our place," said Pip "we always stay in the kitchen Rags and me and I get the bowl and he gets the spoon and the egg beater – Sponge cake's best – it's all frothy stuff then." He ran down the verandah steps on to the lawn, planted his hands on the grass bent forward and just did not stand on his head – "Pooh!" he said "that lawn's all bumpy, you have to have a flat place for standing on your head – I can walk all round the monkey tree on my head at our place – nearly, can't I Rags?" "Nearly!" said Rags faindy. "Stand on your head on the verandah. That's quite flat," said Lottie. "No, smartie," said Pip, "you have to do it on something soft see? Because if you give a jerk – just a very little jerk and fall over like that bump yourself something in your neck goes click and it breaks right off. Dad told me . . ." "Oh do let's have a game," said Kezia – "Do let's play something or other –" "Very well" said Isabel quickly "we'll play hospitals. I'll be the nurse and Pip can be the doctor and you and Rags and Lottie can be the sick people" – But No, Lottie didn't not want to play that because last time Pip squirted something down her throat and it hurt awfully. "Pooh!" said Pip "it was only the juice out of a bit of orange peel –" "Well let's play ladies" said Isabel "and Pip can be my husband and you can be my three dear little children – Rags can be the baby –" "I *hate* playing ladies" said Kezia "because you always make us go to church hand in hand and come home again an go to bed" – Suddenly Pip took a filthy handkerchief out of his pocket – "Snooker, here sir" he called, but Snooker as usual, began to slink away with his long bent tail between his legs. Pip leapt on top of him – and held him by his knees – "Keep his head firm Rags" he said as he tied the handkerchief round Snooker's head with a funny sticking up knot at the top. "What ever is that for" – asked Lottie. "It's to train his ears to grow more close to his head, see" said Pip. "All fighting dogs have ears that lie kind of back and they prick up – but Snooker's got rotten ears they're too soft." "I know" said Kezia, "they're always turning inside out I *hate* that." "Oh it isn't that" said Pip "but I'm training his ears to look a bit more fierce see" – Snooker lay down and made one feeble effort with his paw to get the handkerchief off but finding he could not he trailed after the children with his head bound up in the dirty rag – shivering with misery. Pat came swinging by. In his hand he held a little tomahawk that winked in the sun. "Come with me now" he said to the children "and I'll

show you how the Kings of Ireland chop off the head of a duck."
They held back – they didn't believe him it was one of his jokes,
and besides the Trout boys had never seen Pat before – "Come on
now" he coaxed, smiling and holding out his hand to Kezia.
"A real duck's head" she said. "One from ours in the paddock
where the fowls and ducks are" – "It is" said Pat. She put her hand
in his hard dry one, and he stuck the tomahawk in his belt and
held out the other to Rags – He loved little children. "I'd better
keep hold of Snooker's head, if there's going to be any blood
about" said Pip – trying not to show his excitement "because the
sight of blood makes him awfully wild sometimes" – He ran
ahead dragging Snooker by the knot in the handkerchief.
"Do you think we *ought* to" whispered Isabel to Lottie. "Because
we haven't asked Grandma or anybody have we?" "But Pat's
looking after us," said Lottie.

At the bottom of the orchard a gate was set in the paling fence.
On the other side there was a steep bank leading down to a
bridge that spanned the creek and once up the bank on the other
side you were on the fringe of the paddocks. A little disused
stable in the first paddock had been turned into a fowl house.
All about it there spread wire netting chicken runs new made by
Pat. The fowls strayed far away across the paddock down to a
little dumping ground in a hollow on the other side but the
ducks kept close to that part of the creek that flowed under the
bridge and ran hard by the fowl house – Tall bushes overhung the
stream with red leaves and Dazzling yellow flowers and clusters
of red and white berries, and a little further on there were cresses
and a water plant with a flower like a yellow foxglove. At some
places the stream was wide and shallow, enough to cross by
stepping stones but at other places it tumbled suddenly into a
deep rocky pool like a little lake with foam at the edge and big
quivering bubbles. It was in these pools that the big white ducks
loved to swim and guzzle along the weedy banks. Up and down
they swam, preening their dazzling breasts and other ducks with

yellow bills and yellow feet swam upside down below them in the clear still water. "There they are" said Pat. "There's the little Irish Navy, and look at the old Admiral there with the green neck and the grand little flag staff on his tail." He pulled a handful of grain out of his pocket and began to walk towards the fowl house lazily, his broad straw hat with the broken crown pulled off his eyes. "Lid-lid lid lid-lid lid" he shouted – "Qua! Qua Qua!" answered the ducks, making for land and flopping and scrambling up the bank – They streamed after him in a long waddling line – He coaxed them pretending to throw the grain shaking it in his hands and calling to them until they swept round him close round him quacking and pushing against each other in a white ring – From far away the fowls heard the clamour and they too came running across the paddock, their heads crooked forward, their wings spread, turning in their feet in the silly way fowls run and scolding as they came. Then Pat scattered the grain and the greedy ducks began to gobble – Quickly he bent forward, seized two, tucked them quacking and struggling one under each arm and strode across to the children. Their darting heads, their flat beaks and round eyes frightened the children – and they drew back all except Pip. "Come on sillies" he cried, "They can't hurt, they haven't got any teeth have they Pat – they've only got those two little holes in their beaks to breathe through." "Will you hold one while I finish with the other" asked Pat. Pip let go of Snooker – "Won't I! Won't I! Give us one – I'll hold him. I'll not let him go. I don't care how much he kicks – give us give us!" He nearly sobbed with delight when Pat put the white lump in his arms – There was an old stump beside the door of the fowlshed – Pat carried over the other duck, grabbed it up in one hand, whipped out his little tomahawk – lay the duck flat on the stump and suddenly down came the tomahawk and the duck's head flew off the stump – up and up the blood spurted over the white feathers, over his hand – When the children saw it they were frightened no more – they crowded round him and began to scream – even Isabel leaped about and called out "The blood the blood" – Pip forgot all about his duck – He simply threw it away from him – and shouted "I saw it, I saw it" and jumped round the wood block –

Rags with cheeks as white as paper ran up to the little head and put out a finger as if he meant to touch it then drew back again and again put out a finger. He was shivering all over. Even Lottie, frightened Lottie began to laugh and point at the duck and shout "Look Kezia look look look" – "Watch it" shouted Pat and he put down the white body and it began to waddle – with only a long spurt of blood where the head had been – it began to pad along dreadfully quiet towards the steep ledge that led to the stream – It was the crowning wonder. "Do you see that – do you see it?" yelled Pip and he ran among the little girls pulling at their pinafores – "It's like an engine – it's like a funny little darling engine –" squealed Isabel – But Kezia suddenly rushed at Pat and flung her arms round his legs and butted her head as hard as she could against his knees; "Put head back put head back" she screamed – When he stooped to move her she would not let go or take her head away – She held as hard as ever she could and sobbed "head back head back" – until it sounded like a loud, strange hiccough. "It's stopped it's tumbled over it's dead" – said Pip. Pat dragged Kezia up into his arms. Her sunbonnet had fallen back but she would not let him look at her face. No she pressed her face into a bone in his shoulder and put her arms round his neck –

The children stopped squealing as suddenly as they had begun – they stood round the dead duck. Rags was not frightened of the head any more. He knelt down and stroked it with his finger and said "I don't think perhaps the head is quite dead yet. It's warm Pip. Would it keep alive if I gave it something to drink –" But Pip got very cross and said – "Bah! you baby –" He whistled to Snooker and went off – and when Isabel went up to Lottie, Lottie snatched away. "What are you always touching me for Is a *bel*."

"There now" said Pat to Kezia "There's the grand little girl" –

She put up her hands and touched his ear. She felt something –
Slowly she raised her quivering face and looked – Pat wore little
round gold earrings. How very funny – She never knew men wore
earrings. She was very much surprised! She quite forgot about the
duck. "Do they come off and on," she asked huskily?

## Alice in the Kitchen

Up at the house in the warm, tidy kitchen Alice the servant girl
had begun to get the afternoon tea ready – She was dressed.
She had on a black cloth dress that smelt under the arms, a white
apron so stiff that it rustled like paper to her every breath
and movement – and a white muslin bow pinned on top of her
head by two large pins – and her comfortable black felt slippers
were changed for a pair of black leather ones that pinched the
corn on her little toe "Somethink dreadful." It was warm in the
kitchen – A big blow fly buzzed round and round in a circle
bumping against the ceiling – a curl of white steam came out of
the spout of the black kettle and the lid kept up a rattling jig as the
water bubbled – The kitchen clock ticked in the warm air slow
and deliberate like the click of an old woman's knitting needles
and sometimes, for no reason at all, for there wasn't any breeze
outside the heavy Venetians swung out and back tapping against
the windows. Alice was making water cress sanwitches. She had a
plate of butter on the table before her and a big loaf called a
"barracouta" and the cresses tumbled together in the white cloth
she had dried them in – But propped against the butter dish there
was a dirty greasy little book – half unstitched with curled
edges – And while she mashed some butter soft for spreading she
read – "To dream of four black beetles dragging a hearse is bad.
Signifies death of one you hold near or dear either father husband
brother son or intended. If the beetles crawl backwards as you
watch them it means death by fire or from great height, such as
flight of stairs, scaffolding etc. *Spiders*. To dream of spiders

creeping over you is good. Signifies large sum of money in the near future. Should party be in family way an easy confinement may be expected but care should be taken in sixth month to avoid eating of probable present of shell fish." "How Many Thousand Birds I see". Oh Life, there was Miss Beryl – Alice dropped the knife and stuffed her Dream Book under the butter dish but she hadn't time to hide it quite for Beryl ran into the kitchen and up to the table and the first thing her eye lighted on – although she didn't say anything were the grey edges sticking out from the plate. Alice saw Miss Beryl's scornful meaning little smile and the way she raised her eyebrows and screwed up her eyes as though she couldn't quite make out *what* that was under the plate – She decided to answer if Miss Beryl should ask her what it was – "Nothing as belongs to you Miss" "No business of yours Miss" but she knew Miss Beryl would not ask her – . Alice was a mild creature in reality but she always had the most marvellous retorts ready for the questions that she knew would never be put to her – The composing of them and the turning of them over and over in her brain comforted her just as much as if she'd really expressed them and kept her self respect alive in places where she had been that chivvied she'd been afraid to go to bed at night with a box of matches on the chair by her in case she bit the tops off in her sleep – as you might say. "Oh Alice," said Miss Beryl "there's one extra to tea so heat a plate of yesterday's scones please and put on the new Victoria sanwich as well as the coffee cake. And don't forget to put little doyleys under the plates will you – You did yesterday again you know and the tea looked *so* ugly and common. And Alice please don't put that dreadful old pink and green cosy on the afternoon teapot again. That is only for the mornings and really I think it had better be kept for kitchen use – it's so shabby and quite smelly – Put on the Chinese one out of the drawer in the dining room side board – You quite understand, don't you. We'll have tea as soon as it is ready –" Miss Beryl turned away – "That sing aloft on every tree" she sang as she left the kitchen very pleased with her *firm* handling of Alice.

Oh, Alice was wild! She wasn't one to mind being told, but there was something in the way Miss Beryl had of speaking to her that she couldn't stand. It made her curl up inside as you might say and she fair trembled. But what Alice really hated Miss Beryl for was – she made her feel low: she talked to Alice in a special voice as though she wasn't quite all there and she never lost her temper – never, even when Alice dropped anything or forgot anything she seemed to have expected it to happen . . . "If you please Mrs Burnell," said an imaginary Alice, as she went on, buttered the scones, "I'd rather not take my orders from Miss Beryl. I may be only a common servant girl as doesn't know how to play the guitar." This last thrust pleased her so much that she quite recovered her temper. She carried her tray along the passage to the dining room "The only thing to do," she heard as she opened the door "is to cut the sleeves out entirely and just have a broad band of black velvet over the shoulders and round the arms instead." Mrs Burnell with her elder and younger sisters leaned over the table in the act of performing a very severe operation upon a white satin dress spread out before them. Old Mrs Fairfield sat by the window in the sun with a roll of pink knitting in her lap. "My dears" said Beryl, "here comes the tea *at last*" and she swept a place clear for the tray. "But Doady" she said to Mrs Trout, "I don't think I should dare to appear without any sleeves at all should I?" "My dear" said Mrs Trout "all I can say is that there isn't one single evening dress in Mess' Readings last catalogue that has even a sign of a sleeve. Some of them have a rose on the shoulder and a piece of black velvet but some of them haven't even that – and they look perfectly charming! What would look very pretty on the black velvet straps of your dress would be red poppies. I wonder if I can spare a couple out of this hat –" She was wearing a big cream leghorn hat trimmed with a wreath of poppies and daisies – and as she spoke she unpinned it and laid it on her knee and ran her hands over her dark silky hair. "Oh I think two poppies would look perfectly heavenly –" said Beryl, "and just be the right finish but of course I won't hear of you taking them out of that new hat, Doady – Not for worlds."

"It would be sheer murder," said Linda dipping a water cress sanwich into the salt cellar – and smiling at her sister – "But I haven't the faintest feeling about this hat, or any other for the matter of that," said Doady – and she looked mournfully at the bright thing on her knees and heaved a profound sigh. The three sisters were very unlike as they sat round the table – Mrs Trout, tall and pale with heavy eyelids that dropped over her grey eyes, and rare, slender hands and feet was quite a beauty. But Life bored her. She was sure that something very tragic was going to happen to her soon – She had felt it coming on for years – What it was she could not exactly say but she was "fated" somehow. How often, when she had sat with Mother Linda and Beryl as she was sitting now her heart had said "How little they know" – or as it had then – "What a mockery this hat will be one day," and she had heaved just such a profound sigh ... And each time before her children were born she had thought that the tragedy would be fulfilled then – her child would be bom dead or she saw the nurse going into Richard her husband and saying "Your child lives *but*" – and here the nurse pointed one finger upwards like the illustration of Agnes in David Copperfield – your wife is no more" – But no, nothing particular had happened except that they had been boys and she had wanted girls, tender little caressing girls, not too strong with hair to curl and sweet little bodies to dress in white muslin threaded with pale blue – Ever since her marriage she had lived at Monkey Tree Cottage – Her husband left for town at eight o'clock every morning and did not return until half-past six at night. Minnie was a wonderful servant. She did everything there was to be done in the house and looked after the little boys and even worked in the garden – So Mrs Trout became a perfect martyr to headaches.

Whole days she spent on the drawing room sofa with the blinds pulled down and a linen handkerchief steeped in eau de cologne on her forehead. And as she lay there she used to wonder why it was that she was so certain that life held something terrible for her and to try to imagine what that terrible thing could be – until by and by she made up perfect novels with herself for the heroine, all of them ending with some shocking catastrophe. "Dora" (for in these novels she always thought of herself in the third person: it was more "touching" somehow) "Dora felt strangely happy that morning. She lay on the verandah looking out on the peaceful garden and she felt how sheltered and how blest her life had been after all. Suddenly the gate opened: A working man, a perfect stranger to her pushed up the path and standing in front of her, he pulled off his cap, his rough face full of pity. 'I've bad news for you Mam' . . . 'Dead?' cried Dora clasping her hands. 'Both dead?'" . . . Or since the Burnells had come to live at Tarana . . . She woke at the middle of the night. The room was full of a strange glare. "Richard! Richard wake! Tarana is on fire" – . At last all were taken out – they stood on the blackened grass watching the flames rage. Suddenly – the cry went up, Where was Mrs Fairfield. God! Where was she. "Mother!" cried Dora, dropping onto her knees on the wet grass. "Mother." And then she saw her Mother appear at an upper window – Just for a moment she seemed to faintly waver – There came a sickening crash . . . .

These dreams were so powerful that she would turn over buried her face in the ribbon work cushion and sobbed. But they were a profound secret – and Doady's melancholy was always put down to her dreadful headaches . . . "Hand over the scissors Beryl and I'll snip them off now." "Doady! You are to do nothing of the kind," said Beryl handing her two pairs of scissors to choose from – The poppies were snipped off. "I hope you will really like Tarana" she said, sitting back in her chair and sipping her tea. "Of course it is at its best now but I can't help feeling a little afraid that it will be very damp in the winter. Don't you feel that, Mother? The very fact that the garden is so lovely is a bad sign in a way – and then of course it is quite in the valley – isn't it – I mean it is lower than any of the other houses." "I expect it will be flooded from the autumn to the spring" said Linda: "we shall have to set little frog traps Doady, little mouse traps in bowls of water baited with a spring of watercress instead of a piece of cheese – And Stanley will have to row to the office in an open boat. He'd love that. I can imagine the glow he would arrive in and the way he'd measure his chest twice a day to see how fast it was expanding." "Linda you are very silly – very" said Mrs Fairfield. "What can you expect from Linda," said Dora "she laughs at everything. Everything. I often wonder if there will ever be anything that Linda will not laugh at." "Oh, I'm a heartless creature!" said Linda. She got up and went over to her Mother. "Your cap is just a tiny wink crooked, Mamma" said she, and she patted it straight with her quick little hands and kissed her Mother. "A perfect little icicle" she said and kissed her again. "You mean you love to think you are" said Beryl, and she blew into her thimble, popped it on and drew the white satin dress towards her – and in the silence that followed she had a strange feeling – she felt her anger like a little serpent dart out of her bosom and strike at Linda. "Why do you always pretend to be so indifferent to everything," she said. "You pretend you don't care where you live, or if you see anybody or not, or what happens to the children or even what happens to you. You can't be sincere and yet you keep it up – you've kept it up for years – In fact" – and she gave a little laugh of joy and relief to be so rid of the serpent – she felt positively delighted – "I can't even remember when it started now – Whether it started *with* Stanley or before Stanley's time or after you'd had rheumatic fever or when Isabel was born –" "Beryl" said Mrs Fairfield sharply. "That's quite enough,quite enough!" But Linda jumped up. Her cheeks were very white. "Don'tstop her Mother" she cried, "she's got a perfect right to say whatever she likes. Why on earth shouldn't she." "She has *not*" said Mrs Fairfield. "She has no right *what* ever." Linda opened her eyes at her Mother. "What a way to contradict anybody," she said. "I'm ashamed of you – And how Doady must be enjoying herself. The very first time she comes to see us at our new house we sit hitting one another over the head –" The door handle rattled and turned. Kezia looked tragically in. "Isn't it *ever* going to be tea time" – she asked – "No, never!" said Linda "Your Mother doesn't care Kezia whether you ever set eyes upon her again. She doesn't care if you starve. You are all going to be sent to a Home for Waifs and Strays to-morrow." "Don't tease" said Mrs Fairfield. "She believes every word." And she said to Kezia, "I'm coming darling. Run upstairs to the bathroom and wash your face your hands *and* your knees."

On the way home with her children Mrs Trout began an entirely new "novel". It was night. Richard was out somewhere (He always was on these occasions.) She was sitting in the drawing room by candlelight playing over "Solveig's Song" when Stanley Burnell appeared – hatless – pale – at first he could not speak. "Stanley tell me what is it" . . . and she put her hands on his shoulders. "Linda has gone!" he said hoarsely. Even Mrs Trout's imagination could not question this flight. She had to accept it very quickly and pass on. "She never cared," said Stanley – "God knows I did all I could – but she wasn't happy I knew she wasn't happy."

"Mum" said Rags "which would you rather be if you had to a duck or a fowl – I'd rather be a fowl, much rather."

The white duck did not look as if it had ever had a head when Alice placed it in front of Stanley Burnell that evening. It lay, in beautifully basted resignation, on the blue dish; its legs tied together with a piece of string and a wreath of little balls of stuffing round it. It was hard to say which of the two, Alice or the duck looked the better basted. They were both such a rich colour and they both had the same air of gloss and stain – Alice a peony red and the duck a Spanish mahogany. Burnell ran his eye along the edge of the carving knife; he prided himself very much upon his carving; upon making a first-class job of it – He hated seeing a woman carve; they were always too slow and they never seemed to care what the meat looked like after they'd done with it. Now he did, he really took it seriously – he really took a pride in cutting delicate shaves of beef, little slices of mutton just the right thickness in his dividing a chicken or a duck with nice precision – so that it could appear a second time and still look a decent member of society. "Is this one of the home products" he asked, knowing perfectly well that it was. "Yes dear, the butcher didn't come; we have discovered that he only comes three times a week." But there wasn't any need to apologise for it; it was a superb bird – it wasn't meat at all, it was a kind of very superior jelly. "Father would say" said Burnell "that this was one of those birds whose mother must have played to it in infancy upon the German flute and the sweet strains of the dulcet instrument acted with such effect upon the infant mind – Have some more Beryl. Beryl you and I are the only people in this house with a real feeling for food – I am perfectly willing to state in a court of law, if the necessity arises that I love good food" – Tea was served in the drawing room after dinner and Beryl who for some reason had been very charming to Stanley ever since he came home suggested he and she should play a game of crib. They sat down at a little table near one of the open windows. Mrs Fairfield had gone upstairs and Linda lay in a rocking chair her arms above her head – rocking to and fro. "You don't want the light do you Linda" said Beryl and she moved the tall lamp to her side, so that she sat under its soft light. How remote they looked those two – from where Linda watched and rocked – The green table, the bright polished cards, Stanley's big hands and Beryl's tiny white ones, moving the tapping red and white pegs along the little board seemed all to be part of one united in some mysterious

movement. Stanley himself resting at ease big and solid in
loose fitting dark suit, had a look of health and wellbeing ab
him – and there was Beryl in the white and black muslin di
with her bright head bent under the lamp light. Round l
throat she wore a black velvet ribbon – It changed her – altei
the shape of her face and throat somehow – but it was ve
charming – Linda decided. The room smelled of lilies – the
were two big jars of white arums in the fireplace – "Fiftee
two – fifteen four and a pair is six and a run of three is nine
said Stanley so deliberately he might have been counting shee|
"I've nothing but two pairs" said Beryl, exaggerating he
woefulness, because she knew how he loved winning. Th
cribbage pegs were like two little people going up the roa
together, turning round the sharp corner coming down the roa
again. They were pursuing each other. They did not so muc
want to get ahead as to keep near enough to talk – to kee
near – perhaps that was all. But no, there was one always wh
was impatient and hopped away as the other came up an
wouldn't listen perhaps one was frightened of the other c
perhaps the white one was cruel and did not want to hear an
would not even give him a chance to speak. In the bosom of he
dress Beryl wore a bunch of black pansies, and once just as th
little pegs were close side by side – as she bent over – the pansi
dropped out and covered them – "What a shame to stop then
said she – as she picked up the pansies, "just when they had
moment to fly into each other's arms!" "Goodbye my gir
laughed Stanley and away the red peg hopped – The drawii
room was long and narrow with two windows and a glass do
that gave on to the verandah. It had a cream paper with a patte
of gilt roses, and above the white marble mantelpiece was the l
mirror in a gilt frame wherein Beryl had seen her drown
reflection. A white polar bear skin lay in front of the firepla
and the furniture which had belonged to old Mrs Fairfield w
dark and plain – A little piano stood against the wall with yell

pleated silk let into the carved back. Above it there hung an oil painting by Beryl of a large cluster of surprised looking clematis – for each flower was the size of a small saucer with a centre like an astonished eye fringed in black. But the room was not "finished" yet – Stanley meant to buy a Chesterfield and two decent chairs and – goodness only knows – Linda liked it best as it was. Two big moths flew in through the window and round and round the circle of lamplight. "Fly away sillies before it is too late. Fly out again" but no – round and round they flew. And they seemed to bring the silence of the moonlight in with them on their tiny wings ...

"I've two Kings" said Stanley "any good?" "Quite good" said Beryl. Linda stopped rocking and got up. Stanley looked across. "Anything the matter, darling?" He felt her restlessness. "No nothing I'm going to find Mother." She went out of the room and standing at the foot of the stairs she called "Mother – " But Mrs Fairfield's voice came across the hall from the verandah.

The moon that Lottie and Kezia had seen from the storeman's wagon was nearly full – and the house, the garden, old Mrs Fairfield and Linda – all were bathed in a dazzling light – "I have been looking at the aloe" said Mrs Fairfield. "I believe it is going to flower – this year. Wouldn't that be wonderfully lucky! Look at the top there! All those buds – or is it only an effect of light." As they stood on the steps the high grassy bank on which the aloe rested – rose up like a wave and the aloe seemed to ride upon it like a ship with the oars lifted – bright moonlight hung upon those lifted oars like water and on the green wave glittered the dew – "Do you feel too," said Linda and she spoke, like her mother with the "special" voice that women use at night to each other, as though they spoke in their sleep or from the bottom of a deep well – "don't you feel that it is coming towards us?" And she dreamed that she and her mother were caught up on the cold water and into the ship with the lifted oars and the budding mast. And now the oars fell, striking quickly quickly and they

rowed far away over the tops of the garden trees over the paddocks and the dark bush beyond. She saw her mother, sitting quietly in the boat, "sunning" herself in the moonlight as she expressed it. No, after all, it would be better if her Mother did not come, for she heard herself cry faster faster to those who were rowing. How much more natural this dream was than that she should go back to the house where the children lay sleeping and where Stanley and Beryl sat playing cribbage – "I believe there are buds," said she. "Let us go down into the garden Mother – I like that Aloe. I like it more than anything else here, and I'm sure I shall remember it long after I've forgotten all the other things." Whenever she should make up her mind to stay no longer – She put her hand on her Mother's arm: and they walked down the steps, round the island and on to the main "drive" that led to the front gates – Looking at it from below she could see the long sharp thorns that edged the Aloe leaves, and at the sight of them her heart grew hard. She particularly liked the long sharp thorns. Nobody would dare to come near her ship or to follow after. "Not even my New Foundland dog" thought she "whom I'm so fond of in the daytime." For she really was fond of him. She loved and admired and respected him tremendously – and she understood him. *Oh,* better than anybody else in the world, she knew him through and through – He was the soul of truth and sincerity and for all his practical experience he was awfully simple, easily pleased and easily hurt – If only he didn't jump up at her so and bark so loudly and thump with his tail and watch her with such eager loving eyes! He was too strong for her. She always *had* hated things that rushed at her even when she was a child – There were times when he was frightening – really frightening, when she just hadn't screamed at the top of her voice – "you are killing me" – and when she had longed to say the most coarse hateful things. "You know I'm very delicate. You know as well as I do that my heart is seriously affected and Doctor Dean has told you that I may die any moment – I've had three great lumps of children already." Yes, yes it was true – and thinking of it, she snatched her hand away from her mother's arm for all her love and respect and admiration she hated him. It had never been so plain to her as it was at this moment – There were all her "feelings" about Stanley one just as true as the other – sharp defined – She could have done them up in little packets – and there was this other – just as separate as the rest, this hatred and yet just as real. She wished she had done them up in little packets and given them to Stanley – especially the last one – she would like to watch him while he opened that . . . And how tender he always was after times like that, how submissive – how thoughtful. He would do anything for her he longed to serve her. Linda heard herself saying in a weak voice, "Stanley would you light a candle" and she heard his joyful eager answer "My darling of course I shall" and through he went giving a leap out of bed and drawing the moon out of the sky for her – She hugged her folded arms and began to laugh silently. Oh dear Oh dear how absurd it all was! It really was funny – simply funny, and the idea of her hating Stanley (she could see his astonishment if she had cried out or given him the packet) was funniest of all. Yes it was perfectly true what Beryl had said that afternoon. She didn't care for anything – but it wasn't a pose – Beryl was wrong there – She laughed because she couldn't *help* laughing. –

And why this mania to keep alive? For it really was mania! What am I guarding myself so preciously for she thought mocking and silently laughing? I shall go on having children and Stanley will go on making money and the children and the houses will grow bigger and bigger, with larger and larger gardens – and whole fleets of aloe trees in them – for me to choose from —

Why this mania to keep alive indeed? In the bottom of her heart she knew that now she was not being perfectly sincere. She had a reason but she couldn't express it, no not even to herself. She had been walking with her head bent looking at nothing – now she looked up and about her. Her mother and she were standing by the red and white camellia trees. Beautiful were the rich dark leaves spangled with light and the round flowers that perched among the leaves like red and white birds. Linda pulled a piece of verbena and crumbled it and held up the cup of her hand to her Mother – "Delicious" said Mrs Fairfield bending over to smell – "Are you cold, child are you trembling? Yes, your hands are cold. We had better go back to the house" – "What have you been thinking of" said Linda – "Tell me" – But Mrs Fairfield said "I haven't really been thinking of anything at all. I wondered as we passed the orchard what the fruit trees were like, whether we should be able to make much jam this autumn – There are splendid black currant and gooseberry bushes in the vegetable garden. I noticed them to-day. I should like to see those pantry shelves thoroughly well stocked with our own jam –"

A letter from Beryl Fairfield to her friend Nan Fry.

My darling Nan,

Don't think me a piggy-wig because I haven't written before: I haven't had a moment dear and even now I feel so exhausted that I can hardly hold a pen – Well, the dreadful deed is done. We have actually left the giddy whirl of town (!) and I can't see how we shall ever go back again, for my brother-in-law has bought this house "lock stock and barrel" to use his own words. In a way it's an awful relief for he's been threatening to take a place in the country ever since I've lived with them and I must say the house and garden are awfully nice – a million times better than that dreadful cubby hole in town – But buried – my dear – buried isn't the word! We have got neighbours but they're only farmers – big louts of boys who always seem to be milking and two dreadful females with protruding teeth who came over when we were moving and brought us some scones and said they were sure they'd be very willing to help. My sister, who lives a mile away says she doesn't really know a soul here, so I'm sure we never never shall and I'm certain no body will ever come out from town to see us because though there is a bus it's an awful old rattling thing with black leather sides that any decent person would rather die than ride in for six miles! Such is life! It's a sad ending for poor little B. I'll get to be a most frightful frump in a year or two and come and see you in a mackintosh with a sailor hat tied on with a white china silk motor veil! Stanley says that now we're settled, for after the most ghastly fortnight of my life we really are settled, he is going to bring out a couple of men from the club each week for tennis – on Saturday afternoons – In fact two are promised us as a *great treat* today – But my dear if you could see Stanley's men from the club, rather fattish – the type who look frightfully indecent without waistcoats – always with toes that turn in rather – so conspicuous too, when you're walking about a tennis court in white shoes and pulling up their trousers, every minute – don't you know and whacking at imaginary things with their racquets. I used to play with them at the Club Court last summer – and I'm sure you'll know the type when I tell you that after I'd been there about three times they *all* called me Miss Beryl! It's a weary world. Of course Mother simply loves this place, but then when I am Mother's age I suppose I shall be quite content to sit in the sun and shell peas into a basin but I'm not not not What Linda really thinks about the whole affair, per usual I haven't the slightest idea. She is as mysterious as ever.

My dear you know that white satin dress of mine. I've taken the sleeves out entirely put straps of black velvet across the shoulders and two big red poppies off my dear sister's chapeau. It's a great success though *when* I shall wear it I do not know . . .

Beryl sat writing this letter at a little table in front of the window in her room. In a way of course it was all perfectly true but in another way it was all the greatest rubbish and she didn't mean a word of it. No, that wasn't right – She felt all those things but she didn't really feel them like that – The Beryl that wrote that letter might have been leaning over her shoulder and guiding her hand – so separate was she: and yet in a way, perhaps she was more real than the other, the real Beryl. She had been getting stronger and stronger for a long while. There had been a time when the real Beryl had just really made use of the false one to get her out of awkward positions – to glide her over hateful moments – to help her to bear the stupid ugly sometimes beastly things that happened – She had as it were called to the unreal Beryl, and seen her coming, and seen her going away again, quite definitely and simply – But that was long ago. The unreal Beryl was greedy and jealous of the real one – Gradually she took more and stayed longer – Gradually she came more quickly and now the real Beryl was hardly certain sometimes if she were there or not – Days, weeks at a time passed without her ever for a moment ceasing to act a part, for that is what it really came to and then, quite suddenly, when the unreal self had forced her to do something she did not want to do at all she had come into her own again and for the first time realised what had been happening. Perhaps it was because she was not leading the life that she wanted to – She had not a chance to really express herself – she was always living below her power – and therefore she had no need of her real self – her real self only made her wretched.

In a way of course it was all perfectly true but in another it was all the greatest rubbish and she didn't believe a word of it. No, that wasn't right: she *felt* all those things but she didn't really feel them *like that*. It was her other self, whose slave or whose mistress she was which? who had written that letter. It not only bored – it rather disgusted her real self. "Flippant and silly" said her real self, yet she knew she'd send it and that she'd always write that kind of twaddle to Nan Fry – In fact it was a very *mild* example of the kind of letter she generally wrote. Beryl leaned

her elbows on the table and read it through again – the voice of
the letter seemed to come up to her from the page – faint already
like a voice heard over a telephone wire, high, gushing – with
something bitter in the sound – Oh, she *detested* it today. "You've
always got so much animation B" said Nan Fry – "That's
why men are so keen on you" – and she had added, rather
mournfully – (for men weren't keen on Nan – she was a solid
kind of girl with fat hips and a high colour) "I can't understand
how you keep it up, but it's your nature I suppose." What rot!
What nonsense! But it wasn't her nature at all! Good Heavens! if
she'd ever been her real self with Nan Fry Nannie would have
jumped out of the window with surprise. My dear you know that
white satin dress of mine – Ugh! Beryl slammed her letter case to.
She jumped up and half consciously – half unconsciously she
drifted over to the looking glass – There stood a slim girl dressed
in white – a short white serge skirt – a white silk blouse and a
white leather belt drawn in tight round her tiny waist – She had
a heart shaped face – wide at the brows and with a pointed
chin – but not too pointed —— Her eyes – her eyes were perhaps
her best feature – such a strange uncommon colour too, greeny
blue with little gold spots in them. She had fine black eyebrows
and long black lashes – so long that when they lay on her cheek
they positively caught the light some one or other had told
her – Her mouth was rather large – too large? No, not really. Her
underlip protruded a little. She had a way of sucking it in that
somebody else had told her was awfully fascinating. Her nose
was her least satisfactory feature – Not that it was really
ugly – but it wasn't half as fine as Linda's. Linda really had a
perfect little nose. Hers spread rather – not badly – and in all
probability she exaggerated the spreadness of it just because it
was her nose and she was so awfully critical of herself. She
pinched it with her thumb and second finger and made a little
face – Lovely long hair. And such a mass of it. It was the colour
of fresh fallen leaves – brown and red, with a glint of yellow.

Almost it seemed to have a life of its own – it was so warm and there was such a deep ripple in it. When she plaited it in one thick plait it hung on her back just like a long snake – she loved to feel the weight of it drag her head back – she loved to feel it loose covering her bare arms. It had been a fashion among the girls at Miss Beard's to brush Beryl's hair. "Do do let me brush your hair darling Beryl," but nobody brushed it as beautifully as Nan Fry. Beryl would sit in front of the dressing table in her cubicle – wearing a white linen wrapper – and behind her stood Nannie in a dark red woolen gown buttoned up to her chin – Two candles gave a pointing, flickering light – Her hair streamed over the chair back – she shook it out – she yielded it up to Nannie's adoring hands. In the glass Nannie's face above the dark gown was like a round sleeping mask. Slowly she brushed, with long caressing strokes – her hand and the brush were like one thing upon the warm hair. She would say with a kind of moaning passion, laying down the brush and looping the hair in her hands "it's more beautiful than ever B. It really is lovelier than last time" – and now she would brush again – she seemed to send herself to sleep with the movement and the gentle sound – she had something of the look of a blind cat – as though it were she who was being stroked and not Beryl – But nearly always these brushings came to an unpleasant ending. Nannie did something silly. Quite suddenly she would snatch up Beryl's hair and bury her face in it and kiss it, or clasp her hands round Beryl's head and press Beryl's head back against her firm breast sobbing – "you are so beautiful. You don't know how beautiful you are beautiful beautiful." And at these moments Beryl had such a feeling of horror such a violent thrill of physical dislike for Nan Fry – "That's enough – that's quite enough. Thank you. You've brushed it beautifully. Good night Nan." She didn't even try to suppress a contempt and her disgust – And the curious thing was that Nan Fry seemed rather to understand this – even to expect it, never protesting but stumbling away out of the cubicle – and perhaps whispering "forgive me" at the door – And the *more* curious thing was that Beryl let her brush her hair again – and let this happen again, – and again there was this "silly scene" between them always ending in the same way more or less, and never never referred to in the daytime. But she *did* brush hair so beautifully. Was her hair less bright now? No, not a bit – "Yes, my dear, there's no denying it, you really are a lovely little thing" – At the words her breast lifted, she took a long breath, smiling with delight, half closing her eyes as if she held a sweet sweet bouquet up to her face – a fragrance that made her faint. But even as she looked the smile faded from her lips and eyes – and oh God! There she was, back again, playing the same old game – False, false as ever! False as when she'd written to Nan Fry – False even when she was alone with herself now. What had that creature in the glass to do with her really and why on earth was she staring at her? She dropped down by the side of her bed and buried her head in her arms. "Oh," she said "I'm so miserable, so frightfully miserable. I know I'm silly and spiteful and vain. I'm always acting a part, I'm never my real self for a minute" – And plainly, plainly she saw her false self running up and down the stairs, laughing a special trilling laugh if they had visitors, standing under the lamp if a man came to dinner so that he should see how the light shone on her hair, pouting and pretending to be a little girl when she was asked to play the guitar – Why she even kept it up for Stanley's benefit! Only last night when he was reading the paper – she had stood beside him and leaned against him *on purpose* and she had put her hand over his pointing out something and said at the same time – "Heavens! Stanley how brown your hands are" – only that he should notice how white hers were! How despicable! Her heart grew cold with rage! "It's marvellous how you keep it up!" said she to her false self! but then it was only because she was so miserable – so miserable! If she'd been happy – if she'd been living *her own life* all this false life would simply cease to be – and now she saw the real Beryl a radiant shadow . . . a shadow . . . Faint and unsubstantial shone the real self – what was there of her except that radiance? And for what tiny moments she was really she. Beryl could almost remember every one of them – she did not mean that she was exactly happy then it was a "feeling" that overwhelmed her at certain times —— certain nights when the wind blew with a forlorn cry and she lay cold in her bed wakeful and listening certain lovely evenings when she passed down a road where there were houses and big gardens and the sound of a piano came from one of the houses – and then certain Sunday nights in Church, when the glass flickered and the pews were shadowy and the lines of the hymns were almost too sweet and sad to bear. And rare rare times, rarest of all, when it was not the voice of outside things that had moved her so – she remembered one of them, when she had sat up one night with Linda. Linda was very ill – she had watched the pale dawn come in through the blinds and she had seen Linda – lying, propped up high with pillows, her arms outside the quilt and the shadow of her hair dusky against the white – and at all these times she had felt: Life is wonderful – life is rich and mysterious. But it is good too and I am rich and mysterious and good. Perhaps that is what she might have said – but she did not say those things – then she knew her false self was quite quite gone and she longed to be always as she was just at that moment – to become *that* Beryl forever – "Shall I? How can I? and did I ever not have a false self?" But just when she had got that far she heard the sound of wheels coming up the drive and little steps running along the passage to her door and Kezia's voice calling "Aunt Beryl. Aunt Beryl!" She got up – Botheration! How she had crumpled her skirt. Kezia burst in. "Aunt Beryl – Mother says will you please come down because Father's home and lunch is ready –" "Very well Kezia." She went over to the dressing table and powdered her nose. Kezia crossed over too and unscrewed a little pot of cream and sniffed it. Under her arm Kezia carried a very dirty calico cat. When Aunt Beryl had run out of the room she sat the cat up on the dressing table and stuck the top of the cream jar over one of its ears. *Now* look at yourself said she sternly. The calico cat was so appalled at the effect that it toppled backwards and bumped and bounced on the floor and the top of the cream jar flew through the air and rolled like a penny in a round on the linoleum and did not break. But for Kezia it had broken the moment it flew through the air and she picked it up, hot all over, put it on the dressing table and walked away, *far* too quickly – and airily.

*also available from*
CAPUCHIN CLASSICS

**Green Dolphin Country**
*Elizabeth Goudge. Introduced by Eileen Goudge*
First published in 1935, 1944, *Green Dolphin Country* is an epic tale of
love, courage and selfless devotion, set in the Channel Islands and New
Zealand in the nineteenth century, written with Elizabeth Goudge's
inimitable feeling for the intricacies of human emotions.
"Breathtaking … A long vista of undulating story, with here and
there peaks of volcanic excitement." *Daily Telegraph*

**Potiki**
*Patricia Grace. Introduced by Kirsty Gunn*
*Potiki* is a mesmerizing novel about a coastal Maori community
threatened with resettlement. The danger to their existence in all that
it means to them is mortal, and the outcome dramatic.
*Potiki* won the New Zealand Book Award for fiction.

**Agnes Grey**
*Anne Brontë. Introduced by Isabel Quigly*
First published in 1847, and thought to be based on Anne Brontë's
own experiences, *Agnes Grey* is a milestone in English literature,
offering a wry, penetrating observation of middle-class Victorian
Britain.
"The most perfect prose narrative in English letters." *George Moore*

**The Man Who Loved Children**
*Christina Stead. Introduced by Angela Carter*
*The Man Who Loved Children* is an astonishing account of the
crumbling of an American bourgeois family. Intimate, accurate and
savagely funny, it is also unforgettably moving.
"The whole book is different from any book you have read before.
What other book represents – tries to represent, even – a family in
such conclusive detail?" *Randall Jarell*

**www.capuchin-classics.co.uk**